Soli Deo Gloria!

Eph. 1:17-19

This Dance

Book One
in the
Sisters Redeemed Series

Jerusha Agen

This Dance

© 2013 Jerusha Agen

ISBN-13: 978-1-938092-44-2
ISBN-10: 1938092449

This book is a work of fiction. Names, characters, places, and incidents are either products of the author's imagination or used fictitiously. Any similarity to actual people and/or events is purely coincidental.

Unless otherwise noted, Scriptures are taken from the Holy Bible, New International Version®, NIV®. Copyright © 1973, 1978, 1984 by Biblica, Inc.™ Used by permission of Zondervan. All rights reserved worldwide. www.zondervan.com

Published by Write Integrity Press, 130 Prominence Point Pkwy. #130-330, Canton, GA 30114.

www.WriteIntegrity.com

Printed in the United States of America.

Soli Deo Gloria

Acknowledgements

Firstly, I am enormously grateful to my publisher, Tracy Ruckman, for taking a chance on me and my novel. Thank you for giving me a venue to share my stories and for your patience during this journey to publication.

My undying thanks goes to my family. I thank Josh for his professional input, Matt for challenging me to grow, and Nate for his promotional support. Thanks to Dad for setting an example of godliness and enabling me to pursue my dreams. To Mom, my best friend and greatest fan: I could not have accomplished this and so much more without you. Thank you.

Chapter One

Nye Sanders pressed her lips into a grim line and glanced in the rearview mirror. The white snow that bordered the freeway gleamed back at her. There had been a time when the beauty of the Pennsylvania winter would have filled her with wonder. But this morning, her mood was as frigid as the outdoor temperature, and she put on sunglasses to block the snow-covered scene.

Annoyed with time lost on the icy residential streets, she pressed the accelerator harder. At least the six-lane freeway had been more thoroughly salted after last night's freezing rain. Nye glared at the clock. She refused to be late to negotiations for—

Nye gasped as her tires hit black ice on a curve and started to skid. She slammed on the brakes. The car slid from side to side. Spun out.

She lost control.

Time slowed as the car swung into a 180-degree turn. Gravitational force pulled her toward the door, then away. Her fingers squeezed the wheel, nails bit into her hand.

White. Everything was white.

The force that spun the car sucked the breath out of her lungs. She was a toy. Something awful was playing with her.

Is this what he had felt? She wished she could see him. She tried.

"Dante!" She called his name as the car slammed into the guardrail. She closed her eyes against the impact. A painful crunch.

Force yanked her body again as the car ricocheted into another spin.

It stopped.

Nye slowly opened her eyes and half expected to see shattered glass scattered across her lap. She stared at the intact windshield. The car rested alongside the road, facing the direction she had been traveling.

Air filled her lungs in a sudden, deep breath, as if her body finally determined it would survive. She loosened her death-grip on the wheel, letting the sound of her breathing soothe her tattered nerves. Her hand shook as she removed her sunglasses and began a mental inventory of her condition. A bruise would likely develop from the seatbelt, and her neck was sore, but she didn't feel the degree of pain that would signal a serious injury.

Now for the real damage. Nye grabbed her white scarf from the passenger seat and wrapped it around her neck. She opened the door and stood against the icy wind that slapped her face. Her knees wobbled, almost collapsing under her. She braced her hand against the car as a lightheaded sensation washed over her and clouded her vision. She leaned against the door and closed her eyes.

"Are you okay?"

Nye started and whirled to meet the source of the deep voice.

A tall stranger watched her across the roof of her car. "Sorry. I was behind you when you spun out. Are you hurt?"

"Uh…" Nye's mind seemed to work in slow-motion as she processed what he said. "No, I'm fine."

He smiled. "Good." He glanced down, then back at her. "I see your car wasn't so fortunate."

She stared at him, unable to concentrate on anything other than his smile, which was nothing short of gorgeous. It went well with his broad shoulders and unusual height. If he were standing closer, even Nye at five feet nine would have to tilt her head to see his face. She suddenly realized she was taking inventory and wanted to shake her head in disgust. Maybe she should add a head injury to the list.

His comment finally registered, and she walked around the front of the car, relieved her legs were steady. "Is it bad?"

"Could be worse."

Nye frowned as she looked at the side that had hit the guard rail. A large dent caved in the back door and garish scratches slashed the black paint. Terrific.

"Thank the Lord you didn't get hurt anyway."

Nye turned to counter the religious statement, but the words died in her throat when her gaze collided with his eyes—as deep and rich as a melted pool of chocolate.

"Are you stuck?"

"What?" Nye tried to match the question to her train of thought.

"Your car. Is it in the ditch at all?"

"Oh." A flush of heat filled her cheeks. "I don't think so." She seized the excuse to hide her embarrassment and looked at the car.

He was already heading for the other side of the vehicle, assessing the car's position. "Looks like you're mostly on the shoulder. Back tire's in the snow a bit, but you should get out okay."

Nye sighed. At least she wouldn't have to spend hours trying to extract the car from a snow drift.

He came back and stopped close to her. "I thought for sure you'd end up in the ditch or worse when you spun out like that." He watched a car drive slowly past, its occupants staring at the roadside scene. "That's a nasty curve in this weather."

"Tell me about it."

He turned his dark gaze on her. "It's a miracle you weren't

hurt. Do you want me to call the police or the hospital or anyone?" He reached into his coat pocket and pulled out a cell phone. "You should see a doctor, just to make sure—"

"No, please. That's really not necessary." A twinge of annoyance ran through her at his assertiveness. But it was impossible to stay irritated when he flashed that grin.

"Sorry. Didn't mean to tell you what to do."

Taken aback by how quickly he interpreted her reaction, Nye paused. Maybe she was being unfair. The man was only trying to help. She mustered half a smile. "It's nice of you to be concerned, but I'm fine. And if I need help, I have my own cell." She reached into her pocket for the phone and winced at the pain that flared in her palm when she grasped the cold plastic.

"Are you okay? Did you hurt your hand?"

Nye slowly removed it from her pocket. "I don't know, I—"

Before she knew what he was doing, her hand was cradled in the warmth of his. "You are hurt." He examined the wounds that were beginning to smart as the effects of the adrenaline faded.

Her fingernails had punctured the skin of her palms, and a small amount of blood seeped out the gashes.

"That's pretty bad. You should have a doctor take a look."

Nye was far more concerned with the way her breathing sped up at his touch than she was worried about some minor cuts. She pulled away. "I'm fine." She glanced at his serious face. There was no call for her to be rude. "Thank you for your concern."

He nodded, his brow furrowed.

The only reason she needed to see a doctor was to figure out why she was having such a strong reaction to a perfect stranger. She hadn't even looked twice at any man since Dante. With the thought, a familiar coldness returned, and it wasn't from the wintry gusts. An icy ache gripped Nye's heart. She wouldn't have to worry about being distracted by the man in front of her anymore.

Cullen Chandler did his best to distance himself from the stranded woman. She'd placed distance between them—both mentally and physically. Her reserved but friendly demeanor suddenly chilled. For a moment, some emotion he couldn't read flickered in her eyes. Then a cool detached expression slid into place. Confused, but also curious, he tried to think of a way to prolong their conversation. If he read her correctly, she was working on the opposite problem.

Loose strands of blonde hair whipped against her smooth cheek. She pushed them back, her gaze taking in the few cars that slowly passed. "I suppose we should get out of here before another car skids." She turned those enormous blue eyes on him, and he completely forgot what she said. He was in big trouble.

Her eyes widened a fraction, and she cleared her throat.

The sound snapped him out of his trance. Feeling as though he had just been hypnotized, he scrambled for something to keep her there.

"We should probably call the police and have them document the accident." Not bad. If he didn't get hold of himself, he'd be asking for her phone number next. He couldn't believe he was having such a schoolboy reaction to a woman he'd just met.

She glanced at the dent. "I don't think it's going to be expensive enough to warrant that. Besides," she pulled back the sleeve of her coat to look at her watch, "I have a meeting to get to." She started to walk around her car then paused to look back. "Thanks for stopping."

"No problem. That is quite a dent. You might need insurance coverage. Are you sure you don't want to call the police? I'd be happy to wait with you 'til they get here." He cringed inwardly, hoping he didn't sound as desperate as he felt.

From the driver's side of the car, she nodded. "I really have to go, but thanks. Hope you didn't freeze on my account."

He laughed and waved. "No, not at all."

She got into her car, and he turned to walk to his. Freeze? He had forgotten it was even cold outside. One look from those stunning blue eyes had warmed him thoroughly. Something more than beauty was responsible for burning the image of her eyes into his mind. They were filled with a haunted, mournful expression that dominated her beautiful features and made him hurt for her, a stranger.

He got into his SUV and sat behind the wheel. His phone vibrated in his pocket. He could finally feel the numbness of his cold fingers as he reached for the sleek electronic and looked at the screen: another message from the office—already the fifth that morning.

Cullen glanced up. The woman's car gradually disappeared into the distance. A sinking feeling pressed against his chest. He should have been impulsive enough to ask for her number. She was gone, and he didn't even know her name.

Chapter Two

"The first, Heaven, hath a song, but no man hears;
The spheres have music, but they have no tongue,
Their harmony is rather danced than sung."
–John Donne

"They're waiting for you inside, Ms. Sanders."

Nye tried to ignore the note of reprimand in the secretary's tone as she passed the stern woman's desk and approached the huge wooden doors of a conference room at Sheffield, Inc. She straightened the hemline of her black suit and wished she had time for a stop in the restroom to check her appearance. Not only was she late for negotiations of possibly the most lucrative sale in the history of the Keese, Brinkerhoff, and Akkerman private equity firm, but she was sure her windblown hair made her look like a straggly rag doll.

She wouldn't have time to tend to the cuts on her hands either. On the drive there, she had done what she could with the stinging hand sanitizer she kept in her purse, but the prospect of nonchalantly hiding her injuries for hours was far from encouraging.

Nye took a deep breath and leaned into the heavy door. As the largest corporation to establish a branch in the city of

Harper, the Sheffield Building was designed to impress and intimidate. The conference room was no less than Nye had expected, with a massive table that served as a dark centerpiece.

What she hadn't anticipated was arriving late and unkempt, her associates and the Sheffield representatives already seated to watch her entrance. Swallowing mortification, she fell back on the professionalism that had enabled her to so quickly climb the executive ladder.

She walked to the open chair near the head of the table with a smile as she surreptitiously assessed the Sheffield representatives that lined one side of the table, opposite her co-workers from KBA. The Sheffield employees were the assortment of individuals typically seen in this business—three middle-aged men, two of whom watched her with a mixture of curiosity and disapproval. The third tried to avoid looking in her direction at all.

Nye's gaze fell on the empty seat beside them, then moved to the short, older man seated at the head of the table. Since he was clearly the leader of this group, Nye addressed him. "Good morning." He responded with a skeptical gaze over the rim of his glasses.

"I'm Nye Sanders, manager of KBA. I must apologize for the delay." She was careful not to allow any suggestion of timidity in the apology as she sat to the right of the grim ambassador. "I'm afraid I was actually involved in a bit of an accident." She directed a professional smile at the other Sheffield representatives. "These winter roads really are fun, aren't they?"

A small smile from one of the men was the only reward for her effort.

Nye removed a folder from her briefcase and set it on the table, careful to keep her scarred palms hidden. She opened the file and glanced at her associates seated to her right.

Ted Farley, KBA's lawyer, leaned back in his chair and smoothed his tie—a bit too relaxed, as usual. If only Nye could redistribute some of his laidback attitude to the rest of the team. Renee Larson fidgeted with the cuffs of her sleeves in the manner that Nye had learned to recognize as the associate manager's nervous habit. Next to Renee, assistant manager Randy Mesick shakily ruffled through a folder until papers spilled out. He glanced at Nye with embarrassment as he retrieved the fallen pages.

Nye smiled, hoping to infuse him with the confidence she felt in her associates. While employed at KBA for the past two years, Nye had seen this team in action enough to know there was nothing to worry about. With the possible exception of Ted, Nye's colleagues were competent, hard workers. Unfortunately, they were a bit intimidated by the New York City reputation of Sheffield, Inc. After eight years in the famed city and encounters with the top celebrities in her profession, Nye was glad the mystique that impressive locations and names offered to others no longer had any effect on her.

She glanced at the empty chair across from her. "I see I'm not the only one running behind this morning?"

The stony man at the head of the table gave a curt nod. "Mr. Chandler. He should be here shortly."

Nye nodded, covering her disappointment that the absent member was another male. More men than women were still the norm in this business, but she usually expected larger corporations to be more progressive. Negotiations with such male-dominated businesses could sometimes become difficult when two women, one of whom was the firm's manager, represented KBA.

"Thank you." A deep voice, thanking the secretary, carried into the cavernous room as the door opened. The handsome stranger from the freeway entered, his presence sweeping in like a fresh breeze.

Nye's breath caught in her throat.

He smiled at her associates, one at a time as he walked toward Nye's end of the table.

He headed for the empty seat across from her. Nye tried to swallow.

His gaze met hers. He froze and looked as stunned as Nye felt. To her dismay, he recovered more quickly than she did and flashed that devastating grin as he pulled out the chair. "Hello, again." His dark eyes twinkled. "I guess you made better time than I did."

She gave a polite nod and looked away, hoping to cool the warmth that spread through her veins and would probably reach her face. His smile should be outlawed.

"Ahem." The dour man at the head of the table pointedly cleared his throat.

Nye turned to see him arch a brow in her direction. Mentally thrashing herself, she tried to focus. She hoped it wasn't too late to stop the downward spiral of this meeting, but she had the unnerving sense that she could only cling to the rail of this out-of-control rollercoaster.

The stern man raised a hand to adjust his glasses. "Although some of us appear to be acquainted," he cast a pointed gaze at Nye and the stranger, "allow me to proceed with the customary introductions." He stared at the late arrival's still-present smile. "That is, if you are all quite ready."

The stranger turned his gaze from Nye to the small man beside him. "Oh, of course. I'm sorry I was late."

The little man nodded and ignored Nye to direct his gaze far down the table at Ted, probably the most competent-appearing employee in his chauvinist estimation. "I am Claude Van Vechten, president of the Sheffield, Inc., Harper branch. To my left is seated Mr. Cullen Chandler, our legal representation in these proceedings, followed by …"

Nye's resolve to concentrate collapsed with the news. The handsome stranger was their lawyer? Negotiations for a sale like this could take months, especially if the Sheffield staff proved as difficult as its members appeared. That meant months of meetings, months of sitting across from that smile. If Cullen Chandler's entrance into the room was enough to make her senses reel and send her mind into a state of blind distraction, she wouldn't be able to last a week.

She was being ridiculous. After all the work she had invested to get where she was in this business, she refused to lose it all because of overactive hormones. She was better than that, stronger than that.

She steeled herself for a glance at Cullen, only to find his gaze fixed on her. She darted a look toward the much less dangerous face of Claude Van Vechten and forced herself to concentrate on the little man's droning voice. Now all she had to do was salvage these negotiations from their disastrous start and squelch her reaction to Cullen. Both tasks seemed impossible as long as she sat across from the man who inexplicably threatened to overturn her precariously-balanced life.

Cullen couldn't help but notice the natural grace of Nye's walk as he followed the KBA representatives out of the boardroom. He wasn't sure if it was Nye or the change of air after being in a closed room for three hours that enlivened his senses.

Admittedly, observation of Nye had been Cullen's

primary occupation during most of the meeting. He hadn't even surreptitiously kept up with messages from his office as he usually did, despite his phone's frequent vibrations. Nye was enough of a distraction on her own.

If he wasn't so pleased to see her again, Cullen might have felt guiltier that his performance as legal counsel hadn't been up to his usual standards. But after his depressing drive, which he had spent kicking himself for not getting the mysterious beauty's name, his glee when he saw her at Sheffield couldn't have been greater. He had thought he'd never meet her again, and then there she was. He had grinned like a Cheshire cat with a tuna fish sandwich through the rest of the session, no doubt looking like an idiot.

His smile faded now, as Nye finished talking to her associates and started down the hallway. Partway through the meeting, he had the idea that he could ask her to lunch. As long as it wasn't technically a date, such an invitation would fit within the legal ethics code he had to follow amid business negotiations. Unfortunately, he hadn't been able to come up with a plausible excuse for inviting her on anything but a date.

He started to follow her at a distance as she headed for the elevators but halted. Maybe he shouldn't ask her. Though he had been overjoyed to see her at Sheffield, she hadn't seemed quite as thrilled. Her tense demeanor reminded him of a wild animal ready to bolt at the slightest provocation. Yet, he caught her watching him twice. She had quickly glanced away, as if embarrassed, but something in her eyes at those moments made him believe the interest and attraction he felt wasn't one-sided.

He started forward but at a much slower pace. Nye pressed the button for the elevator. The last thing he wanted to do was scare her away, but he felt a crazy need to talk to her, to find out everything about her. The elevator doors opened. She stepped inside.

He rushed forward. "Hold the—"

The ring of his cell phone stopped him. He grimaced and reached into his pocket as the elevator doors closed. No chance the electronic saboteur would work on an elevator for once.

"Hey, buddy." Grant Walker's voice, usually a welcome sound, echoed numbly in Cullen's ear.

"Grant. How are you?"

"It's Friday! Hey, I know you're probably busy, so I'll make this quick."

"Shoot." Cullen put Grant on speaker and navigated to check his email on the phone.

"Sherry and I want to invite you to dinner tonight. I know it's short notice, but if you don't have any plans…"

Tension crept into Cullen's shoulders as he scanned the long list of messages from the firm.

"That's really nice of you, Grant. I wish I could, but I'm really swamped here."

"Work?"

"What else?"

"It's Friday night, Cullen."

Cullen tried to hide his irritation as he nodded to Claude Van Vechten and the other Sheffield representatives who passed on the way to the elevators. Cullen would've thought his law school pal and fellow attorney would understand the pressures of the legal profession. "Yes, I know. I'm working with a partner on a deal that's closing this weekend."

"Isn't that like the sixth weekend in a row you've worked?"

"I don't know. I'm not keeping track." He opened another message on the phone and scanned the contents. "You know how it is."

"Not really."

Cullen sighed. "Not now, Grant." He was not in the mood to rehash Grant's reasons for why Cullen should get out of corporate law and use his skills for something more "worthwhile"—like the public defense Grant enjoyed so much.

"Okay." Grant's tone signaled his intention to return to the topic at a later time. "How about dinner tomorrow night?"

"Can't. No, not work," Cullen added, before Grant could protest. "I'm hoping to visit Granddad."

"Oh, that's great. It's been a while since you were out there, hasn't it?"

Cullen winced as Grant's question hit the bull's-eye of his conscience. "Yeah."

"Well, at least you're doing something other than work." Grant paused. "Not that there's anything wrong with working hard. I just wonder if—"

"Sorry, Grant, but I really have to run." The additional projects assigned to Cullen in the messages were not putting him in the frame of mind for a lecture—even one from a concerned friend.

"Are you checking your messages while we're talking?"

Cullen paused for a moment, wishing he could say no. "Yes."

"That's pathetic, man. You can't even stop working for two minutes."

"Can you save the lecture for another time? I'm on the clock right now."

"Yeah, yeah, I got it. You're still going to make it to church on Sunday, right?"

"Of course." He couldn't hide the note of hurt in his response. Did Grant really think Cullen wouldn't make time for church?

"Pick you up at eight?"

"Right. See you then." Cullen dropped the phone into his pocket as he walked to the elevators and punched the button. *Come on. Could the elevators move any slower?* The interruption from Grant had killed time Cullen couldn't spare. At this point, each new assignment he received felt like a block of cement added to a pack that would eventually crush him under its weight. Maybe he didn't have the temperament for this job, or maybe he just didn't enjoy the realization that he would have to skip lunch again. It was a good thing he hadn't asked Nye out after all.

The thought of the tall beauty was a welcome distraction, enough to soften some of the tautness that had infused his neck and shoulders. A smile wandered onto his face just as two elevators opened at the same time. Grinning at his own immaturity, he chose the elevator that she had taken.

His pleasant thoughts were interrupted by the vibration of his phone. Sure, it would work on an elevator this time. Cullen scrolled through the extensive list of messages and located the newest one that likely contained another task to finish before sundown. He looked at his watch: one fifteen and his work had only begun.

Nye heaved a sigh as she entered her office. What a day. After hours locked in battle with three obdurate men and her equally obstinate emotions, Nye felt more drained than she ever had from a day in private equity. Her ability to remain emotionally detached from her job and clients usually left her with a bottomless supply of energy to perform her duties in an objective, clear manner. Today, she experienced the exhaustion that people who passionately threw themselves into this business must go through every day.

The clock on the wall signaled it was only one thirty. Great. She had hoped it would be much closer to the end of the business day. Her small reserve of energy waned as she reached for the chair and swiveled it toward her.

"I wouldn't bother sitting down yet." Brianna Larson walked through the doorway, lips pursed in the focused expression that always seemed so out of place on her delicate features. Nye normally appreciated Brianna's concentration, since it made her an excellent and reliant secretary, despite her youth. At the moment, however, Nye wished the promising young woman wasn't quite so ready to announce the next tasks to be done.

"Is your phone dead or something?"

"I don't think so. Why?" Nye reached for her purse and pulled out the oversized smartphone she secretly despised. The screen was dark. She pressed the power button.

"I sent you a couple messages. Thought you'd want to head out to Russell Flanagan's property right from Sheffield."

"He won't deal over the phone?" The low battery icon flashed on the phone. "Drat." She set the electronic device on the desk. "Dead battery."

Unfazed, Brianna nodded. "Said he wants to see the person who's trying to buy his land."

"That wouldn't really be me, but okay." Resolving herself to the task, Nye picked up her purse and phone. "Directions?" She headed for the door.

"Here." Brianna handed Nye papers with the Flanagan file as she passed. "Estimated drive time twenty-five minutes." She followed Nye into the hallway. "There were several messages from—"

"Hold up, Nye."

Nye turned.

Dan Akkerman, the youngest principal at KBA, strode toward her. "Hot date?"

"What?"

He tapped his watch. "You're skipping out early." His eyes held a teasing glint.

"Sorry to disappoint, but I'm going to see Russell Flanagan."

He raised his eyebrows.

"We're hoping to buy his property. Just outside Harper …"

"Oh." Dan nodded, his expression dismissive. "I'm glad I caught you anyway. How'd it go with Sheffield?"

Nye covered her surprise at the question. Even though Dan was overseeing the sale of KBA's portfolio company to Sheffield, Nye thought he would maintain his usual disinterest in details of the firm's operations. She tried to respond with greater optimism about the sale than she felt. "It might be more difficult than we had hoped, but I'm sure we'll work it out."

He smiled. "Of course. You always come through. Think it'll take long to close?"

"It could. The representatives are a bit more inflexible than I expected."

A frown, something rarely seen on Dan's face, appeared. "Uh-huh." He paused and looked away. When he glanced back, his trademark grin was in place. "You'll beat 'em, Nye. Have fun playing hooky." He started to back up in the direction he came. "Don't do anything I wouldn't."

She shook her head and turned to Brianna.

The competent secretary held out Nye's coat with a sympathetic look.

"Thanks. I'll plug in my phone in the car and call you on the way." Nye headed for the exit, her fatigue dragging like another heavy garment as she opened the door and faced the cold.

Chapter Three

"Let Israel rejoice in their Maker;
Let the children of Zion be joyful in their King.
Let them praise His name with the dance…"
–Psalm 149:2

Nye pushed her freezing fingers into the warmth of her coat pocket as she raised her other hand to knock once more. Her knuckles hit the door with the force of her impatience. Russell Flanagan was apparently not home, despite Brianna warning him of this visit.

Nye turned and scanned the snow-covered land that sprawled in front of the house. A wooden fence lined both sides of the long, unplowed driveway. Tire tracks from her car marked the only disturbance to the picturesque scene—a winter vision of the kind she used to adore. As she squinted against the sunlight that reflected off the white powder, the emptiness of the fenced pastures looked desolate and lonely, not beautiful. The silence that surrounded her was like the sound of death and loss, not peace. She walked toward the steps that led off the porch.

"Leaving already?" A man approached from the side of the house, using crutches to walk without his right leg, which came to an abrupt end at the knee. He made his way up a shoveled path, glancing at Nye as he went.

Nye stared as he adeptly used the crutches to surmount the short set of steps.

He moved with such confidence that she thought better of offering to help. He reached the top and crossed the porch.

As he neared, Nye could see he was much older than he had appeared from his athletic movement. Perhaps he could be the eighty-two-year-old man she had come to meet. The skin of his face was weather-beaten, worn with age, and he hunched over the crutches. Though clearly not the towering man he probably once was, he still stood taller than Nye.

She cleared her throat, wishing she had been informed of his handicap. "You must be Russell Flanagan."

"Yes, ma'am." He took off his tattered baseball cap, revealing thinning white hair. He leaned on his crutches and extended his free hand. "Welcome to Flanagan Ranch."

Nye grasped his warm hand, feeling as if she had suddenly landed in a scene out of an old western, complete with a sweet-talking cowboy. She was distracted from the image by the strange, rigid feel of his hand in hers.

As he replaced his cap, Nye noticed his swollen knuckles and severely stiffened fingers.

"Sorry I didn't hear you. I was out in the barn. What's a pretty young lady like you doing all the way out here?"

"I'm Nye Sanders from Keese, Brinkerhoff, and

Akkerman. I believe my secretary mentioned I was going to stop by?"

He peered at her. "Oh, shoot. You aren't that buyer are you?"

Her professional smile faltered slightly. "Well, we are interested in your land."

"And here I thought you were too pretty to be another one of those." A teasing sparkle lit his dark brown eyes making Nye do a double take.

There was something familiar about those eyes.

"Well, no sense in you standing out here in the cold. Come on in, and we'll get a hot cup of coffee." He turned quickly and swung his crutches in front of him, heading for the door.

Nye followed, trying to gather her thoughts and come up with a new plan of attack. Russell Flanagan might have severe arthritis and a missing leg, but he was hardly the defenseless, feeble old man she had expected to see. She had the feeling that if she didn't stay on her toes, this grandfatherly cowboy would rope her with his charm before she got a chance to talk him into anything. Not used to feeling vulnerable with a property owner, Nye cautiously followed him into the house. Warmth engulfed her as she stepped inside and closed the door.

He took off his cap and hung it on an ornate, wooden coat rack that was mounted on the wall. "Hang your coat there if you like." He continued down the short hallway and disappeared through a doorway on the right.

Nye glanced at the empty hooks of the elegantly crafted rack. Mr. Flanagan hadn't worn a jacket outside. She shook her head. How had his hand been so warm against her frigid one? Still cold, she opted to keep her coat.

She glanced around, taking a moment to study the parts of the house she could see. When she began her business career, Nye had learned to capitalize on her natural ability to read people. Examining a subject's appearance and behavior could tell her a lot about that individual's personality and desires. She could then devise a negotiating strategy tailored to persuade that specific person and obtain her objective. She was given a rare opportunity in the Flanagan case—she was getting inside his house, his personal living space.

A framed photograph of a beaming bride and groom sat on a small, intricately-carved table near the door. Perhaps his son or daughter? Beside the picture was a small basket that held a cluster of snapshots, most taken with a Polaroid camera. Knowing better than to paw through them, she just noted the top one—two young boys wearing cowboy hats sat on the back of a huge, brown horse.

Nye walked a few steps and glanced through the doorway on her left. The medium-sized living room was homier than she would have expected from the widower she had read about in Flanagan's file. The knickknacks and handmade doilies that decorated the room bore witness to the enduring influence of his deceased wife. A large painting of a church hung above an unlit fireplace.

"Lost out there?"

The gravelly sound of Flanagan's voice jerked Nye out of her investigation. She went to the doorway on the right and entered a kitchen the color of sunbeams. The cabinets, table, and chairs—all skillfully crafted from a pale-toned wood—enhanced the warmth of the decor. Nye squelched the urge to smile at the sight of this masculine cowboy surrounded by bright, daisy stenciled walls, as he removed two mugs from a cupboard.

He leaned on a crutch to turn and face Nye. "This room was my wife's. Told her she could do it up anyway she'd like, and she did."

Nye blinked at him. She thought she had covered her amusement.

His smile told her he had managed to read her thoughts anyway. "Daisies were her favorite."

Nye nodded. "It's lovely." She hoped a polite smile would hide her disconcertment. She didn't like the feeling that he could see right through her.

He set a crutch against the counter and dug in his pocket. He pulled out what looked like a worn piece of paper and crossed the space between them using only one crutch.

Nye's mouth dropped open at the age-defying display. The one-crutch maneuver might be feasible for a young amputee, but she doubted many men of eighty-two could pull it off.

"Here she is."

Nye looked at the photograph he held out to her. The wallet-sized image, worn on the edges, showed a silver-haired woman, her high cheek bones and sparkling eyes marks of a great beauty, aged with time.

"Gloria." He said the name like an endearment. As he looked at the photo, his mouth angled into a smile.

"You must miss her a great deal."

"I do." He nodded and gently slid the picture into his pocket. "But she had a full life. The Lord gives, and the Lord takes away. Blessed be the name of the Lord."

"Job." Nye couldn't keep the irritation completely out of her voice.

He looked at her with curiosity, but not surprise. "You know the passage?"

"Well enough." She supposed it was easy for him to mouth religious platitudes, maybe even believe them. At least his wife had lived a "full life," as he put it. Maybe it had been her time to die. Everyone had to die eventually. But not when all of life was still to be lived. Not like Dante. The cold ache gripped her heart. She had to get back on track.

"I'm sorry, Mr. Flanagan. Here you're probably waiting for me to get to the point, and I'm asking about your family."

"Nonsense." He turned and went to the whistling tea kettle on the stove. "Don't get many visitors these days. What'd you say your name was?"

"Nye Sanders."

"Nye. Thought it was something different. How'd your folks come up with that?"

"They like unique names. It means 'island dweller.'" Nye offered, before he asked the inevitable follow-up question. "Nothing special."

"Sounds special to me. Coffee?"

"That would be lovely. Thank you." Her inward cringe denied the words. Oriana would say she was being a coffee snob, but Nye just couldn't stand the instant version of her favorite drink these days. Convincing a property or business owner to accept a purchase offer often required sacrifices along the way. She had to connect with the owner on a personal level, and refusing this man's hospitality was not likely to accomplish that objective.

"Can I help?" Nye watched in amazement as he carried the two mugs to the small table in one hand, again using only one crutch.

"Nope." He set the mugs down. "You just have a seat." He headed back for the tea kettle.

She removed her coat and pulled out a chair, setting her briefcase on the floor.

He returned with the tea kettle and poured steaming water

into the mugs. "You take cream or sugar?"

"No, thank you."

"Well, I'll be." He looked up with a pleasantly surprised smile on his face. "Don't think I've ever met a woman who likes her coffee black."

"We're not all alike."

He threw back his head and laughed—a deep, hearty rumble that made Nye want to smile in response. "Don't I know it." He removed the spoon from her coffee and pushed the mug toward her. Still smiling, he slid into the chair opposite hers. "My Gloria used to tell me that all the time. Never could keep myself from making assumptions, I guess. At least that's what she always said."

Nye returned his smile. "Well, I have to admit I probably got my taste for strong coffee from my father. He never likes a hint of anything sweet in his."

He lifted his mug in salute. "A man after my own heart." He took a sip, then looked at Nye with a searching gaze. "So why do you want to buy my ranch?"

Nye nearly sputtered the coffee she was drinking. How had she let herself get caught so off-guard? Somehow this man had distracted her so thoroughly that she was talking about her family, breaking her cardinal rule to never mix her personal life with business. No matter—she would recover quickly enough. She was just upset that she had let herself get charmed into such a position. This was definitely not her best day. "I didn't realize you were operating a ranch here," she answered, implying a question that he would have to address, giving her time to refocus.

"I guess I'm not really. Not anymore. Used to own quite a few horses."

"You don't anymore?"

"No, ma'am. Couldn't afford to keep 'em."

Nye searched for a sign of sadness or remorse in his face, but saw a smile instead.

"We used to have some beautiful quarter horses. You like horses?"

"I haven't had much experience with them."

"Well, if I still had old Betsy, we'd take care of that right now. She was Gloria's mare. A real sweetheart, but I don't have her anymore, so I guess God's got something else in mind."

Hiding her discomfort at his inclination to bring religion into the conversation, Nye tried again to get back to business. "I'm sorry you weren't able to afford the horses. I understand financial concerns are the reason you've placed your property up for sale?"

He nodded. "City decided to take over my ranch— annexing, I guess they call it. Now they want me to put in a whole mess of stuff I don't have the money to pay for. Sidewalks, sewers—"

"It must be very upsetting." Nye didn't usually have to dig

to find the property owner's bitterness in a case like this. She could sometimes use that resentment to fuel the negotiation by taking on the role of a sympathetic friend there to offer comfort and monetary compensation for the victim's hardship. But no anger furrowed this man's brow or flashed in his eyes.

Afraid he was about to spout another Bible quotation, she started her spiel. "I can't save your property for you, Mr. Flanagan, but I would like to do what I can as far as compensating for your loss. The firm that I represent is prepared to offer you a tremendous deal, a very substantial sum for your land."

"Do I look like a fellow who's interested in money?" He fixed her with a steady gaze.

"No, you don't, but there are certainly a number of things you could do with more money. Things that could help make your life more comfortable. You could easily afford arthritis medication, perhaps even purchase a wheelchair, if you'd like."

He cracked a smile. "You're a sharp cookie. My daughter and grandkids have been trying to get me into a wheelchair for years. They say I'm stubborn, but I compromised." He grabbed the crutch that leaned against the table and waved it with a grin. "I use two of these now." He looked at her for a moment. "You know, the last fellow who came out tried to tell me I could get one of those plastic legs with the money. As if I couldn't have done that years ago if I'd wanted."

Nye wasn't surprised other buyers had already been there.

His large spread lay right on the fringes of Harper's extending city borders. What had once been a peaceful section of country acreage was being surrounded by new businesses, making it a prime piece of property for developers. "May I ask who else you've talked to?"

"A couple of boys wanting to build a casino here." His lips pressed into a thin line. "Won't have any of that. What are you going to do with my land if I sell to you?" He narrowed his eyes, but kept a steady glare on her.

She smiled, trying to make him relax. "My firm won't build on or use the land for anything directly." Caught under his shrewd gaze, she opted for honesty. "In this case, we would hold the land until we found another buyer."

"You know the folks who'd buy it from you?"

Nye hesitated. "We have a few interested parties, but I'm not free to say who they are."

He looked down. "I see."

The wrinkles on his forehead deepened, and he clasped his stiff hands together.

"I don't want to rush you at all, Mr. Flanagan. There's no need to make a decision right now." She reached into her briefcase and pulled out some paperwork. "I've taken the liberty of bringing a preliminary contract with me." She set it on the table in front of him. "The details of this offer are flexible, so if there's anything you object to, talk to me, and I'm sure we'll be able to arrange it more to your liking."

He leaned over the document, squinting at the words. He glanced up. "I don't have my glasses with me."

Nye smiled. "Oh, no, Mr. Flanagan. I'm going to leave this copy with you. I'll give you some time to think about it and call you next week."

He shook his head. "I don't like to do business over the phone."

"Then I'll stop by. Is Monday all right?"

"I expect I'll need more time to pray about it."

Of course. Nye stifled her annoyance. "That's perfectly fine. Take all the time you need, have your lawyer look it over and—"

"Don't have a lawyer."

She paused. "Oh. You may want to get one for these proceedings."

"Why? You planning to cheat me?"

Nye was relieved to see the twinkle in his eyes. "Of course not, but there will be a lot of technical legal jargon in this contract and other documents. I want to make sure there isn't anything in our offer that you're unaware of."

"Well, I appreciate that. But I'd imagine you can answer any questions I'll have."

"Of course, but should you decide to take an offer from anyone else, you'll want a lawyer in case—"

"Don't you worry about other offers. I'm only looking at yours right now."

She forced a smile. "I'm glad to hear that." Why was she trying so hard to make sure he had legal representation? It wasn't any of her business if he didn't want to be protected. She normally had no problem staying out of other people's business. Perhaps Russell reminded her too much of her grandparents, who had all passed away by the time she graduated from college.

No, that explanation didn't seem like enough. Somehow, she felt as if she had already known this sweet man for a long time. Most prospective buyers would have leapt for joy at his admission that he didn't have legal counsel. Yet the thought of him being vulnerable to anyone, even to her own highly polished business skills, broke through Nye's usually implacable detachment from business matters.

She was bothered enough that, moments later, as she unlocked the door to her car and slid into the cold interior, she wondered if she should have tried harder to convince Russell to get a lawyer.

She shook her head and turned the key in the ignition. What was wrong with her? Two negotiations in one day had threatened to strip her of all defenses and make her break every one of her rules regarding emotional detachment and the separation of business from personal life. The accident on the highway must have shaken her more than she had thought. She wouldn't … she couldn't consider any other explanation.

Chapter Four

*"All which is not itself the Great Dance was made
in order that He might come down into it."*
–C. S. Lewis

Nye was glad for something to do, even if it was just stirring pasta, as she finished telling her sister the selective recap of her wild car ride that morning. She braced herself for the overreaction.

"Are you okay? Were you hurt?" Oriana looked up from the lettuce she held under the faucet and stared at Nye, her brown eyes wide.

Nye shouldn't have told Oriana about the traffic accident, but her younger sister was always too good at detecting when Nye was trying to hide something. The alarm on Oriana's face was enough to make Nye wish she had at least tried to keep the event a secret. She didn't want stress or worry to ruin this rare chance for the two of them to eat dinner together.

"I'm fine." An annoying prick of conscience made her feel like she had to say something more honest. "Well, except for a few scratches on my hands."

"Let me see." Oriana plunked the head of lettuce on the

counter and leaned close to see the injuries. She gasped. "Nye, you shouldn't be doing anything with those hands! Why didn't you bandage them?"

Nye rolled her eyes as Oriana led her by the arm, away from the counter. "I wasn't about to walk into the Sheffield negotiations with huge, bandaged clubs for hands."

Oriana pulled Nye to the table and pushed her into a chair. "Stay there. I'm getting the first aid kit."

Nye laughed. "Good grief, Oriana. It's not that serious."

Oriana pointed at Nye. "Stay."

The huge German shepherd that slumbered by the table raised his head.

"Not you, Jordan," Oriana added as she turned and disappeared down the hall.

Nye smiled in spite of her exasperation. It didn't take much to bring out Oriana's mothering instincts these days. The troubled kids she taught for a living occupied her mind so much that her teacher persona was never far away. Despite the mothering, Nye missed spending time with her sister. Considering that they shared a house together, they saw surprisingly little of each other. Oriana's teaching kept her busy during the week, but she usually had free evenings and weekends. Nye was the reason they didn't often do much together. She typically had work to catch up on or deals to close.

According to Oriana, Nye created the extra work herself,

out of a desire to keep busy. Nye didn't see anything wrong with that, if it were true. Staying busy was healthy. She did miss her lengthy chats with her sister, though, and Nye was determined to spend more time with her this weekend. It just happened to be an added bonus that doing so might be a good distraction from thoughts of the Sheffield deal.

Oriana reappeared with the kit and sat across from her sister. "Okay, put out your hand."

Nye felt like one of Oriana's pupils. As her sister gently applied ointment to the scratches, her brow furrowed in concentration.

"This might hurt a little." Oriana bit her lip.

"I think I'll be able to handle it."

Oriana glanced up, a smile relieving some of the worried lines on her face. "Sorry, I didn't mean to mother. Force of habit." She looked back down at her work. "But you really need to take better care of yourself, Nye. Thank the Lord you weren't more seriously hurt. You probably wouldn't have gone to the hospital."

Thank the Lord. The words sounded so foreign, so strange. Cullen had said them, too. Three years ago, Nye would have said the same thing herself. Now her cynicism railed against the phrase. Why thank God? So He hadn't killed her in the accident. Maybe He hadn't even cared enough to notice she'd been in one. It didn't matter. She'd rather have died out on that highway than have gone through the kind of suffering

God had already inflicted upon her. That winter weather, another thing she had once loved, would be the instrument of bringing pain into her life was a predictable irony.

"There. Now, you might heal properly." Oriana looked at Nye's bandaged extremities, admiring her handiwork.

"Right. Thanks."

Oriana gave Nye a searching look. "Are you okay?"

"Sure. Just thinking." Nye wasn't about to share any of her thoughts on the subject of God. Oriana still clung to the beliefs instilled by their parents. Fortunately, Oriana also knew Nye well enough to sense when it was not a good time to question her. "The pasta needs stirring."

Oriana shot Nye a firm glance when she stood. "You stay put. I'll finish the salad." She went into the kitchen.

Too tired from the day's events to argue, Nye relaxed in the chair and watched Oriana continue to prepare the meal.

"So, how did the Sheffield meeting go, anyway? I know you said it's a big deal for your firm."

Nye groaned. So much for avoiding that topic. "Don't even ask."

Oriana glanced at Nye. "Was it really that bad?"

"Well, I ended up being late because of the accident, and then I had to face a panel of sour-faced men representing Sheffield."

Oriana laughed.

"And then who should walk in but the guy who—" Nye

caught the slip too late.

Oriana stopped stirring the pasta and pinned Nye with a stare. "What guy?"

Nye wanted to kick herself. She had purposefully left out any mention of Cullen in her story of the accident. "A man stopped to check if I was okay after my car spun out." She tried to act casual but couldn't help the heat that rose to her face.

Oriana walked closer to the table and stared at Nye. "He stopped. And you talked to him?"

"Just briefly."

"And then he was at the meeting?"

Nye could almost see the wheels turning in her sister's mind. She met Oriana's searching gaze with a blank expression. "Turns out he's the lawyer representing Sheffield."

"I see. This lawyer must've made quite an impression."

"Not at all. It was nice of him to stop, but I wouldn't have given him a second thought if he hadn't shown up at the meeting." Not quite true, but Nye had to do something to protect herself.

Oriana gave her a sly look. "And I suppose that's why you tried so hard to avoid mentioning him."

Nye couldn't help the smile that tugged at her lips. "Goodness, you're persistent."

"So?" Oriana's eyes sparkled with barely contained excitement.

"So maybe I did notice, in passing, that he was good-looking." Maybe maintaining a placid expression would sell the gross understatement. She wasn't about to give her sister a more accurate description when she already looked so gleeful.

Oriana squealed and practically bounced over to the table. Jordan sprang to his feet, eagerly watching.

Nye held up a bandaged hand to prevent Oriana's hug and countered her enthusiasm with a stern gaze. "I just said he was good-looking. That doesn't mean a thing."

Oriana laughed. "Nye, you've always had cute guys hanging around you. Except for Dante, you never even seemed to notice. I don't care what he looks like, but the fact that you noticed him means there's something special about—"

"No!" Nye looked away, trying to calm her impassioned breathing. She reigned in her rising emotions and met Oriana's startled gaze. "It doesn't mean anything." Nye said the words calmly, but with a gravity that she hoped would make them sink in. "We're professional associates on a business deal. That's all. You should know nothing else can come of it."

"I won't stop hoping, Nye." The softness of Oriana's voice reached for Nye's deadened heart.

Nye looked away. "It would be better for both of us if you did."

Cullen pushed away from his desk. It was the third time in the last hour that he had caught himself thinking of Nye when he was supposed to be getting work done. He rose from the leather chair and went to the window. The Venning and Henderson law firm occupied the top floors of the State Bank skyscraper, and his office offered a great view. Until this week, it hadn't really mattered that the windows provided a bird's eye perspective of a certain Keese, Brinkerhoff, and Akkerman private equity firm. Now, the presence of the quiet brick building pressed relentlessly on Cullen's mind.

He gazed at KBA's snow-covered roof and wondered if Nye was there right now. He shook his head at the train of thought. What was it about this woman? He had never in his life reacted this way to anyone. As he watched the white city below, the irrepressible grin return—that goofy smile that had overtaken his face for the duration of the meeting at Sheffield. He couldn't help it. It was a gift from God that he had been able to find out more about Nye and had the promise of seeing her throughout these negotiations.

Even so, after spending three days in a state of distraction, Cullen was convinced it was for the best that he hadn't been able to ask Nye to lunch after the meeting. Not only had he avoided scaring her off, but he also got a much-needed opportunity to regain some perspective. Without the lunch, Nye had still found her way into his dreams the past few nights, leaving him baffled as to the reason why. Yes, she was beautiful, but physical attractiveness alone would never have had him tossing and turning as he slept.

The intensity of his emotions for this woman frightened him. He had to get some distance—get his feet back on the ground. He reminded himself that he hardly knew anything about her. He didn't even know if she was a Christian.

With that thought dousing the excited flares in his mind, he turned back to the desk, sighing at the stacks of papers covering its surface. A tremendous workload that constantly demanded eighty-hour work weeks may be common in the legal profession, but he didn't enjoy spending Saturday afternoon at the office, especially when he had planned to visit his grandfather.

Cullen's gaze sought the old snapshot of his grandfather with Buck, a prized quarter horse. He spotted the framed picture wedged between the piles that waited for his attention. Maybe he could find time to call tonight if he got home early enough. At least then he wouldn't have to feel so badly that he had even told Grant he was going to visit.

"Ah, Chandler. Excellent."

Cullen looked up with a start to see Harris Blanchard, a partner at Venning and Henderson, stride through the open doorway.

Blanchard's face, slightly ruddy under a receding line of graying hair, transformed dramatically with his emotions, revealing his thoughts and attitudes almost completely to anyone watching. For most lawyers, such expressiveness would probably be a hindrance. But Blanchard managed to use even that characteristic to his advantage. Incurring the partner's displays of wrath or disapproval ranked among the greatest fears of the staff and associates at the law firm. Blanchard's overpowering personality was one of many aspects of the firm that Cullen hadn't discovered until after he transferred there.

At this moment, Blanchard's expression transitioned from pleasure at seeing Cullen in the office on a Saturday to disapproval, likely because he wasn't seated at the desk, hard at work.

"Gordon Franklin changed his mind about the working capital adjustment. I need you to revise the purchase agreement. Get it to me by five."

Cullen nodded, knowing Blanchard wouldn't give him a moment to say anything.

"With this client, I wouldn't be surprised if we can't close the deal until Monday. You'll be here tomorrow?"

Cullen opened his mouth to reply, then shut it when Blanchard abruptly turned and marched out of the office. Blanchard's tone transformed his question into a statement of fact—an expectation that couldn't be disappointed.

Cullen raked a hand through his hair just as his cell phone rang. Glad it hadn't sounded when Blanchard was still there, Cullen picked it up to check the caller ID. Grant. It was past office hours. Cullen should be free to answer his own phone if he wanted. With a little surge of defiance and a glance at the empty doorway, he lifted the phone to his ear. "Hi, Grant."

"Hey. Let me guess, at the office?"

Cullen rolled his eyes as he sat in his chair. "Let me guess, you're at home?"

"You got it. Went out to lunch, had an epic snowball fight with the kids, and now I'm just reading a good book, putting my feet up in front of the fire."

Cullen grinned. "You don't have a fireplace."

"Are you sure? You've only been here once."

Sensing some truth behind Grant's ribbing, Cullen braced himself. "Is that why you called by any chance?"

"Well, I know I caught you at a bad time yesterday, so I thought I'd call you on your alleged day off and try again."

"For what?" Cullen tapped a key on his keyboard to wake the computer out of stand-by mode.

"Dinner. Tonight. I know you said you're going to visit your grandfather so bring him with you. I'd love to meet him."

"I'd like that, too, but—"

"It's spaghetti and meatballs…"

Cullen had to smile at the enticing way Grant dangled the words. "Sounds great, but it looks like I won't be able to get away tonight."

"From your grandfather?"

Cullen swallowed. "No."

"Work." Judging from the tone of Grant's voice, he was not pleased.

Cullen stared at the computer screen in the silence.

"Do you remember why you said you wanted to move here?"

Cullen blinked. He hadn't expected the question. "There were a lot of contributing factors." He was stalling, and Grant was smart enough to know it.

"Let me tell you what I remember. I remember a guy telling me he was sick of the work-is-everything mentality at the firm in Philly. A guy who said he was tired of running for his life under the partners' thumb and worrying every day that he was going to lose his job if he didn't work twenty-four seven. You said you didn't want to keep fearing you would never make partner or would get fired unless you killed yourself to keep up. Am I right?"

"I had other reasons, too, but, yes, those were some of them." Cullen shifted uncomfortably in his chair.

"Oh, yeah. The other reasons: you wanted to move to a smaller city and be closer to your grandfather, neither of which you've seen because of work."

Cullen tried to remember why he was friends with a lawyer. "I'm new at the firm, Grant. You know how that is. I have to make a good showing."

"For how long? You've been here a year."

"Ten months."

"Okay." Grant's volume lowered as he calmed down. "Look, I'm just worried about you. You haven't been able to commit to a church or anything yet."

"You know I was trying to give Community more time to work out."

"Yeah." Grant paused. "Just ... can you honestly say things are any better at Venning than they were in Philly?"

Cullen tried to think of an answer that wasn't a lie. He couldn't deny that he felt pressured and still worried he might get fired, especially since Blanchard had singled out Cullen as some sort of victim or testing ground from day one. "They did agree to let me have Sundays off here," he lamely offered, acknowledging to himself that Blanchard didn't really respect that agreement.

"But you can't do dinner tomorrow night, either, can you?"

Grant knew Cullen way too well. "I have to work somewhere, Grant." Cullen propped his elbow on the desk and rested his forehead in his free hand, the week and the argument taking its toll.

Perhaps knowing his friend had felt enough heat, Grant sighed. "Okay, buddy. Try to get some rest tonight, if you can."

"Thanks."

"See you at church tomorrow?" Grant's cautious tone suggested he was starting to question if he'd said too much.

"I'll be there." They'd been friends too long for Cullen not to recognize and appreciate the concern behind the badgering. As they said good-bye, Cullen looked at the clock, trying not to be bothered by how much further behind the phone call had put him. In truth, he was more discouraged by the facts Grant had made him face.

It wasn't better here, but maybe things weren't better at any law firm anywhere. It didn't really matter at this point. Cullen was no quitter. He had to do his best in the profession he'd chosen, and he had already run away once. If he could just hold on long enough to make partner, things would get better then. Making partner had always been his goal, and there was a better chance of that at Venning than at the massive firm in Philly.

Cullen blew out a breath. His wayward thoughts were not helping him get to partner any faster. He sat up straighter and flipped open the file for the Sheffield deal.

The lovely vision of Nye at the meeting appeared involuntarily in his mind—a welcome change, but still another distraction. He shook his head and shoved the folder aside. Grabbing the file for Franklin's purchase agreement and setting it next to the keyboard, he pulled up related information on the computer, determined to concentrate. Now if his emotions would just show some respect for his better judgment, he might manage to get a few hours' sleep before church in the morning.

Chapter Five

"The joy of our heart has ceased;
Our dance has turned into mourning."
–Lamentations 5:15

"Nye …"

A voice slowly forced its way through the thick, sleep-induced fog in Nye's head.

"Nye, you promised you'd go to church with me today, remember?"

A tug on the blankets. A bright light tried to push through Nye's closed eyelids.

"If you don't wake up in five seconds, I'm gonna sic your dog on you. One … two …"

"Oohhh." Nye's groan pushed past her dry lips as she recognized Oriana's voice.

"… three… four, five! Get her, Jordan!"

"Ooofff!" Nye gasped for air as her one-hundred-pound German shepherd crushed her beneath him. "All right, all right! I'm awake!" Nye laughed and hugged her furry friend.

"Whose idea was it to get up this early anyway, huh, boy?" Nye asked Jordan, as she ruffled the fur on his neck.

"Mine!" Oriana piped up cheerfully from the end of the bed. "And you only have fifteen minutes 'til we leave, so you better hurry."

"Fifteen minutes!"

"Sorry." Oriana threw an unapologetic smile over her shoulder as she went to the door, waving the Danish she carried in her hand. "That's what happens when you ignore your alarm clock."

Ugh. Cheerfulness like that before morning coffee was disgusting. Nye pushed away the bed covers and let her feet sink into the plush, carpeted floor. She shuffled to the connecting bathroom, followed by the soft jingle of dog tags. She turned and bent to kiss Jordan on top of his head. "You stay here, boy. I'll be out in a bit."

He gazed up at her face with his large, dark eyes and obediently slid down on the floor to lie where she indicated.

"Good boy." Nye smiled as she gently closed the door. She reached into the shower to turn on the water, and her smile faded as she thought of what was ahead of her.

She hadn't set foot in a church for three years, and she didn't want to now. She had only agreed to go because Oriana made such a huge deal out of needing her to help serve refreshments for the church's twentieth anniversary open house. Nye peeled off her pajamas and stepped into the shower, letting the spray massage the tension out of her shoulders. Though this was a different church than the one that held so many painful memories for her, it still had entirely too much to do with the God she had tried to forget.

So much for her brilliant ideas. Nye had purposely slowed her morning preparations in the hope they would arrive at church late enough to warrant sitting in a back pew. No such luck. Oriana was determined to sit next to their parents in her "regular" place: the fifth pew from the front of the large sanctuary. Now the situation was ten times worse, with the entire congregation already in place when Nye and Oriana arrived. No doubt they would all stare at Nye and wonder why she hadn't been there before since she lived with her sister. She nervously glanced at the backs of their heads. What exactly had these people been told about her?

"Staring at them won't make them go away, you know." Oriana returned from hanging up her coat and stood beside Nye.

Nye glared at her.

"Are you ready to go in now?" The twinkle in Oriana's eyes belied the sincere tone of the question.

After another dark look for Oriana, Nye braced herself to enter a church sanctuary for the first time in three years.

Clouds of memory engulfed her as she followed Oriana to the front. The sound of the organ, the soft murmuring of the congregation interrupted by an occasional cough, the colored

sunlight that streamed through stained glass windows—
everything reminded her of Dante. As she sat in the pew next to
Oriana, Nye felt Dante at her side.

She turned to look. A sting of pain shot through her when
her gaze fell on the fabric of the empty space beside her.

She couldn't do it. Nye jerked to her feet, not caring who
saw as she rushed up the aisle, barely stopping herself from
breaking into a run. She reached the lobby, her breathing
ragged as she looked through blurred vision for a retreat.

Some people stopped talking and stared.

Nye spotted the women's restroom and rushed to the door.
She stumbled to a bench just inside and sank onto it. Covering
her face with her hands, she breathed, trying to calm the
swirling memories in her head. She could hear Dante, the last
time they had attended a service together, talking about how
much he loved church architecture.

"It reminds me why art is so important," he had said. "The
things people create, like this church and even our dancing—
it's all reflecting God's glory. Isn't that incredible?" The inner
joy that always amazed her had emanated from his smile as he
put his arm around her shoulders, and they had turned together
to listen to the prelude music.

Nye lowered her hands and straightened, taking deep
breaths. From where had his joy come? Nye had been a
Christian for as long as she could remember, but other than
when she was with Dante, she never felt anything like the

complete peace and contentment she saw in his eyes. No, even with him she had never possessed anything like that. She had often imagined that his inner joy came from his love for her. But she had questioned that belief more than once.

If not from love, then what? God? It couldn't be, or Nye would have felt the same thing. If God could give such joy, he wouldn't have taken Dante. He wouldn't have taken her dancing, her life, her soul.

Nye stood and went to the mirrors that lined the wall above the sinks. Digging in her purse, she pulled out a lipstick tube. As she applied the subtle color, she saw a familiar coolness in her eyes, as if the chill of her heart was reflected in her gaze.

She looked away. She would stay for the anniversary celebration as promised, but she wouldn't set foot in the sanctuary again. Dante was wrong. God created beauty only to destroy it. Nye would have to be daft or suicidal to have anything to do with a God like that. As of this moment, she was neither.

Nye glanced up at the sound of her mother's voice. It came from the foot of the church basement stairs, where the ever-popular Caroline and Marcus Sanders paused to talk to friends.

Nye sighed, relieved by the temporary delay. Her parents

were carrying trays laden with desserts for the table she was setting up, so she only had a moment to brace herself for the inevitable. She felt a twinge of guilt as she watched her parents. They're wonderful people, and I love them, she reminded herself.

She pursed her lips and rearranged some plates on the table, remembering a time when she had a healthy relationship with her parents. Even when she had left to attend college in New York City, Nye had remained especially close to her mother and chatted with her on the phone almost every day. Like everything else in her life, Nye's relationship with her mother died with Dante.

Nye's parents hadn't known Dante very well since he also lived in New York, and they couldn't begin to understand what Nye went through when he was killed. They disapproved of her decision to quit dancing, change careers, and leave her friends. It seemed her mother viewed everything about the way Nye chose to live her life as wrong. That disapproval felt like a noose tightening on Nye's neck whenever she was around her parents. The only method she had devised for dealing with the situation was to avoid them as much as possible—no easy task when they lived only ten minutes from Nye and Oriana.

The avoidance tactic was hopelessly flawed for scenarios like the one that Nye faced now. Her parents broke away and headed for her table. Where was Oriana anyway? Nye glanced around. She usually depended on Oriana's presence to diffuse the tension.

"Hi, sweetie!" Mother smiled as she approached.

"Hey, stranger." The pleased glint in her dad's eyes told Nye he didn't mean any criticism.

Guilt curdled in Nye's stomach at her own, negative attitude. With an effort to act more her age, she forced a smile. "Hello, Mother. Dad." She reached across the table to take a couple plates off the tray her mother carried. Noticing her favorite dessert as she set the dishes on the table, Nye glanced at her mother. "Mmm. Your chocolate cheesecake looks as good as ever."

"Thanks, sweetie."

"I'm going to have a hard time sticking to one slice."

Mother removed the rest of the plates from her tray, and transferred them to the table. "You should have a couple. You're looking thin. You aren't skipping meals at work again, are you?" She moved the desserts around, rearranging the display to meet her idea of perfection.

Dad smiled at her. "I think she looks terrific."

She gave him a grateful glance.

Her mother glanced at him. "Of course she does. You know I just meant … well …" She turned to Nye. "You look tired, that's all." She walked around the table to give Nye a hug. "But it's lovely to see you. We've missed you."

Oriana breezed over to the table.

Nye stifled a sigh of relief and stepped back from her mother. Childish or not, she felt as if she had just been rescued.

"How are we doing? Everything set up? I'm going to get the rest of the food and stuff, okay?"

Nye blinked at her sister. Oriana's already high energy level often vamped up to greater extremes when she was in charge of an event like this.

"Good, yes, and go to it!" Her mother laughed.

"Great. Nye, can you serve the punch?"

"What? I'd rather—" Nye's attempted protest fell on deaf ears as Oriana whirled away and disappeared up the stairs.

Dad chuckled. "I still can't figure out where she got all that energy."

A middle-aged woman approached the table, her gaze focused on Mom.

Mom smiled. "Beverly! How are you? How was the luncheon?"

Dad winked at Nye. "Well, maybe it isn't that hard to figure out."

Nye couldn't help the tug at her lips. Her dad always had a knack for bringing a smile to her face, even when she was feeling far from cheerful.

He sobered. "How are you doing, really?"

Nye donned a blank expression. "Great. How are you?"

Mother leaned in. "Nye, could you fill a couple glasses for Beverly and her husband?"

"Hello, there, Marcus." A man Nye assumed was Beverly's husband clapped her dad on his shoulder, pulling him into a conversation.

Nye reluctantly lifted the ladle and started to serve the growing line of people waiting for punch.

She was here. Cullen jerked to a halt on the staircase, unable to believe his eyes. But the tall blonde-haired woman who stood behind a table serving punch was undoubtedly the one who had appeared in his dreams. Nye Sanders was the last person he had expected to see. He must have missed her during the service because he had sat with Grant's family only a few rows from the front.

Harper was a small city, but it seemed unbelievable that they would again meet unexpectedly. The sense of the hand of Providence at work gave Cullen hope that there was some legitimate reason for what he was feeling. After another fitful night of sleep, thanks to Nye, Cullen had been growing increasingly puzzled and preoccupied. He had caught Grant giving him several strange looks this morning. Grant knew Cullen well enough to tell when something was bothering him, but he probably thought it was their conversation the day before.

Something was bothering Cullen, all right, and she stood before him, lovelier than he remembered. How could her image be so constantly in his mind and yet the real thing be even more beautiful? There was one thing that was the same—that sadness. The haunted gaze. It made him want to promise her things: that everything would be all right, that he wouldn't let anything happen to her, and that he'd fight off the pain that gripped—

"Oh! Excuse me!"

Someone bumped into him from behind. Embarrassed to realize he was still standing on the staircase as he stared at Nye, he turned.

A friendly smile met his apologetic one as a brunette peered at him over a large cardboard box. "I'm sorry. I didn't see you standing there." Her eyes shown with a curious glint as she shifted the box and kept her gaze on his face.

He smiled, trying to hide his chagrin. "Don't be. It was my fault." He glanced at the box when she adjusted her hold on it again. "Can I help you with that?"

"No, thanks. I need the exercise. It looks like we're going to run out of potato chips, so I had to grab some more from my car."

He raised an eyebrow. "That whole box is for chips?"

She laughed. "No, I also brought ginger ale for another batch of punch."

"I could take the ginger ale to the punch table for you," he offered, immediately thinking of Nye's location.

"Oh, thanks." She smiled. "That'd be great." She lowered the box so he could reach in and grab the three bottles. "I've never seen you at our church before. Is this your first time here?"

He smiled at the implication that she knew everyone in the church. Judging by her outgoing friendliness, he believed it. "Yeah, I came with some friends. I'm new to Harper and haven't found the right church home yet." Saying he was new might be a stretch, but he didn't want to explain that he had only stayed so long at Community because his parents had gone there, years before.

"Well, I hope you like it here. My name is Oriana."

"I'm Cullen. Nice to meet you."

"You, too." She smiled again and walked around him. "And thanks for your help."

She went to the snack table on the opposite side of the room from the punch, but Cullen scarcely noticed. His attention was already diverted to the woman he hardly knew but thought about much more than he should. The butterflies in his stomach made him feel as if he was back in eighth grade and about to ask the most popular girl in school to dance with him. Wow, he really needed to get a grip. He sighed as he realized that, at least where his heart was concerned, the advice was already too late.

Nye mustered a weak smile as another person came for punch from her dwindling supply. Of course, Oriana would give Nye the job with the most people contact. Nye was tired of these strangers' curious glances and attempts to make conversation. She would much rather be curled up on the couch at home with Jordan, a good book, and a mug of hot coffee. That was one wish she would have to keep to herself. If Oriana heard her say it, Nye would be subjected to yet another lecture on her anti-social behavior of late. Oriana was mostly bothered, Nye supposed, because she hadn't always been that way. She was never as outgoing as Oriana, but Nye had often attended parties and social gatherings, which she actually enjoyed, without having to force a friendliness she didn't feel. Another time, another life.

Nye sighed and looked up as another person approached the table. Her heart nearly stopped when her gaze met the handsome face of Cullen Chandler.

"Hello." His deep voice and the slow smile that angled his mouth was enough to make any woman weak in the knees. "I didn't expect to see you here."

"Wha …" Her voice came out in a whisper, and she stopped to clear her throat. "What are you doing here?" Nye barely stifled the urge to smack herself on the forehead. What kind of a question was that? She sounded like she owned the place. She couldn't believe the effect this man had on her. No one else had the ability to reduce her mind and social capabilities to mush with one little smile.

That culpable feature grew larger. "I'm looking for a different church to attend. The Walkers said they really like it here, so I came with them. Grant Walker is an old law school buddy of mine. Maybe you know him?"

"Uh, no." Nye mentally shook herself out of the dreamy spell cast by his smile. Good grief. What was wrong with her? "I don't normally attend this church, either."

"Really, are you here with friends?"

"My sister." Nye nodded in the direction of the snack table. "Oriana."

"Oriana?" Cullen glanced over at the friendly brunette who eyed them. "I met her on my way downstairs. That's where I got these, actually."

Nye noticed he was carrying three bottles of ginger ale. She also realized that because the area around the punch bowl was filled with desserts, he couldn't set them down. "Oh, I'm sorry!" Heat spread up her neck, and she was sure her face was fast approaching the color of the pink punch. She pushed some dessert plates closer together to clear space for the ginger ale.

"Thanks." He placed the bottles on the table as Oriana came over with Hawaiian Punch, the other ingredient needed for another batch.

"Whew! This is a bigger turnout than I thought we would have." Oriana blew out a breath of air as she pushed a wave of dark hair away from her face. "How are you doing over here?"

Although the question was directed at Nye, Oriana tilted her head and glanced at Cullen.

She better not get any ideas. Nye tried to telegraph a warning to Oriana via a meaningful gaze.

Oriana smiled sweetly in return and waited for an answer to her question.

"Great." Nye forced an equally innocent smile. Out of the corner of her eye, she saw Cullen watching them. If they'd been sitting across from each other at a table, she would have been tempted to give Oriana a good kick for making her embarrass herself again.

"Thanks for bringing the ginger ale over," Oriana said to Cullen.

"No problem. Can I help you mix it?"

"You've done enough already," Nye spoke up, determined to stop Oriana from slipping into matchmaking mode.

"Please? I'd like to help." He looked like a little boy asking for one more cookie.

Nye's heart lurched.

"Of course you can help." Oriana shot Nye a look that discouraged anything she might have said. "Would you want to get the orange and pink lemonade concentrates from the freezer in the kitchen?"

"And the kitchen would be …" He turned away from the table to look.

Oriana pointed to a doorway next to the snack table. "Over there, on the right."

"Got it."

He walked across the room with a relaxed, confident stride, a natural grace in his movement. Nye wondered if he had ever taken dance lessons. Shocked at her thoughts, she sucked in a sharp breath. She hadn't thought about dancing for so long. She was getting better. She didn't need to live and breathe dance anymore. Nye refused to believe her stability was that fragile—so weak that meeting one handsome guy could erase years of arduous progress.

"Wow." Oriana's breathless comment drew Nye's attention back to her sister.

"What do you mean, 'wow'?" Annoyed with herself, Nye's question came out sharper than she intended.

"He is some hunk. And don't pretend you didn't notice. I saw you drooling after him."

"I was not drooling," Nye protested, a little too emphatically. Alarmed at the gleam in Oriana's eyes, she added, "Don't go and set me up on a date with him. I am not interested in anyone. Not." She repeated the word more to remind herself than Oriana.

"It seemed like you got along well, anyway," Oriana backtracked. "You acted like you knew each other. Have you met him before?"

Nye cringed. Was it too much to wish her sister wasn't so inquisitive? "He's the guy I told you about," she murmured.

"What?" Oriana stared at Nye. "The one at the accident? The lawyer?"

Nye nodded.

"That's him? You called that guy 'good-looking'?" Her voice was incredulous. "Good grief, Nye! He looks like he stepped off the cover of GQ. He's gorgeous."

"All right, all right. People will hear you." Nye checked nervously for her parents. She spotted her mother, fully engrossed in a conversation, oblivious to Oriana's exclamations. Somewhat relieved, Nye shot a glance toward the kitchen where Cullen emerged carrying the concentrate. She lowered her voice. "So maybe I wasn't quite accurate in my description."

Oriana emitted an unladylike snort.

"I just didn't want you to get excited." She looked firmly at Oriana. "Gorgeous or not, I'm still not interested."

Nye turned to meet Cullen's ice-melting smile. She swallowed and wondered if she could believe her own words.

Cullen set the concentrate on the table, feeling the gazes of Nye and her sister.

"Why don't you two go mingle a bit while I mix the punch?" Oriana offered. "Poor Nye has been stuck behind this table for a while."

Nye shot her sister a sharp glance. "I don't mind staying here."

What was going on between those two?

"No, really, I insist." Oriana smiled.

Nye spotted Cullen watching them and immediately calmed her features, making her expression unreadable. She walked out from behind the table. "Okay. Thanks."

A delectable-looking dessert caught Cullen's eye. "Maybe I'll have one of these as a reward for all my hard work." He thought his heart would stop completely when Nye actually smiled. He had never seen a real smile from her before, and he wasn't sure he could take it if she ever did it again. When she smiled like that, the sadness in her eyes vanished, and she became even more beautiful than before.

"Go ahead." She laughed softly.

He grabbed two plates of cheesecake and lifted one toward her. "Care to join me?"

She looked from the cheesecake to his face and back again as if he had offered her something far more dangerous than dessert. "Sure, I guess I could."

He studied her as they walked away from the table, and she took a bite of chocolate cheesecake, her face relaxing with pleasure. It was a good look—one he hadn't seen her wear since he'd met her. He wondered again what caused the haunted expression that was so often at the back of her gaze.

Uh-oh. The object of his study had caught him staring and now watched him curiously. He stifled a groan. Perhaps if he said something quickly he could avoid looking like a gaping schoolboy. "How are your hands?"

"Oh, they're recovering, thanks." She glanced at the hand not holding her plate. "Oriana's taking good care of them. I think she only let me go without bandages today because we were running late for church."

"She seems like a great sister."

"She is." Nye's gaze drifted toward Oriana, cheerfully serving punch.

"Do you get to see each other much?"

Nye turned back to Cullen. "Not as much as I'd like, but we do share a house."

"Oh, really? Here in Harper?"

"Yes."

"Have you lived in Harper long?"

She nodded. "I grew up here, actually. I lived out of state for a while, but I've been back for a couple years. How about you?"

"I moved here about ten months ago." He was not going to exaggerate it into a year, as Grant liked to do. "But I knew Harper from when I was a kid."

"Really?" She lifted her eyebrows.

"Yeah. My brother and I spent a few summers here at my grandparents' place."

"The rest of your family lives elsewhere?"

"Philadelphia. That's where I was raised. I always enjoyed my time here. It's such a change from Philly. So quiet and peaceful. Seems like a smaller city than it is."

"I know what you mean. I was glad to move back."

"Where did you live when you were away?" He asked the question casually, but glanced up in time to see her body tense.

"I went to college in New York and worked there after I graduated." Though her voice remained normal, sadness returned to her eyes.

Her sudden change in demeanor increased his curiosity. "New York City?"

She nodded.

What was so bad about living in New York? He carefully ventured another question. "What did you major in?"

She didn't answer for a moment. Then, "Dance."

Amazing. With that one simple word, her complexion paled, and her eyes acquired a vacant, unreadable look. Not wanting to press her any further on a topic that for some reason distressed her, he put another forkful of cheesecake in his mouth and chewed slowly.

She looked down at her dessert plate for a moment. When she lifted her gaze, her color and expression had returned to normal. Whatever was bothering this mysterious beauty, Cullen was fascinated by her incredible ability to control her emotions.

Nye desperately wished for more control over her emotions as she struggled to force her thoughts onto a different path. "How long have you been representing Sheffield?" She held her breath as she waited to see if he noticed her obvious attempt to change the subject.

He looked at her with nothing but innocent friendliness reflected in his gaze. "They've been one of my clients since I moved here." He grinned. "But don't let that throw you. I think I've still managed to stay a pretty nice guy."

She smiled. "So I've noticed." Nye almost gasped. Was she actually flirting? This had definitely gone too far. But a tingle still moved down her spine when his gaze warmed and a twinkle appeared in his eyes. She swallowed and wondered how she could escape.

"There you are."

Saved by … her mother? Nye's momentary relief turned to a new kind of tension when her pseudo-savior came over to them.

"I was looking for you, Nye." She smiled at Cullen as she spoke.

Nye fought a groan as her mother shook Cullen's hand.

"Oriana tells me you helped Nye the other day. It was very kind of you. I didn't even know she had been in an accident."

The noose tightened as she shot Nye a pointed glance.

"Oh, I didn't do anything." He waved away the commendation. "I happened to see the accident, and I just checked to make sure she was okay. That's all."

"Well, that's still more than most people would've done." She studied him with a warm gaze. "So what brings you to our church today?"

Nye cringed inwardly as the questioning began. Mother hen found a potential mate for one of her little chicks, and there would be no stopping her now. Her mother would think Cullen was wonderful. There was nothing for her not to like. It wouldn't matter at all that Nye wasn't looking for romance.

Nye glanced at Cullen, who was answering one of her mother's questions. Nye's breath caught when she saw him watching her. She didn't know how to interpret the peculiar glint in his eyes, but she did know it made her uneasy. Most likely because of the way it made her knees wobble and her breathing grow ragged. No. She did not want a romantic relationship of any kind, now or ever again.

Nye sank into the driver's seat with a deep sigh.

Oriana buckled her seat belt. "Well?" She watched Nye from the passenger side.

"Well, what?" Nye started the car and backed out of the stall, glad she was doing the driving. At least she had an excuse not to face her sister, though she could still feel Oriana's inquisitive stare.

"How'd it go?"

"Well, after Mom grilled him for half an hour, I learned all sorts of things." Nye kept her voice light, but she gripped the steering wheel. "He's single, lives in an apartment downtown, and was raised in a good church. Oh, and he has an older brother who's married and has two kids."

Oriana laughed. "Is that all?"

Nye wished. Unfortunately, their mother had also shared with Cullen much of the same information about Nye. At least they were on an even playing field. But what game were they playing? If her mother had her way, Nye and Cullen would be dating by next week. What Nye feared had happened: her mother loved Cullen, or at least loved the idea of him as a match for her daughter. The choking sensation had been worse than normal, as her mother had turned her approving gaze away from Cullen to send Nye meaningful looks.

Trying to make light of the situation in the hope she would feel better about it herself, Nye glanced at Oriana. "I think our dear mother is definitely smitten." Nye pulled the car out of the lot and onto the street.

Oriana chuckled. "She's not the only one."

Nye swallowed. "What do you mean by that?"

"I saw the way he was looking at you. Did he ask you out?"

Nye's mouth dropped open, and she looked at her sister.

Oriana stared back at her. "What?"

Nye jerked her head away to watch the road. "Good grief, Oriana! I've only met the man twice."

Oriana shrugged. "He couldn't take his eyes off you the whole time. The guy is definitely a goner."

Nye ignored the way her stomach did a little cartwheel at that possibility and tried to concentrate on reality. "I'm sure you were just seeing what you wanted to see."

"Ha!" Oriana smirked. "It wasn't just Cullen, either. Don't think I didn't notice how you were struggling to even smile at anybody until he showed up."

Nye threw her a sharp glance.

"Yes, you. You even talked to him for an hour."

An hour? Had it really been that long?

"Admit it, Nye. You like him."

Nye frowned. "Why can't you respect the fact that I don't want that kind of relationship?"

"You don't want any kind of relationship."

"That's not true, and you know it."

"Isn't it?" Oriana's voice tightened. "Do you have any friends at work? Or anywhere? I don't get it. Is it because of what happened with your old friends? That guy … Nicanor?"

Nye's anger flared at the reference. "My personal life is my business, Oriana. Leave it alone. You're acting like Mother."

"No, I'm not." Oriana's tone warned she was trying to

hold back tears. "Mom thinks you need to find another guy to be happy. I don't." She sighed. "I don't mean to pry. It's just … the first time you mentioned Cullen to me and when you talked to him today, I saw something I haven't seen for a long time."

Nye stared at the road, refusing to take the bait.

"I saw happiness in your eyes. Not much, but a glimmer. I haven't seen that since—"

"That's enough."

"Nye! Why won't you just admit it? I don't understand what would be so bad about being interested in Cullen. What happened to Dante is not going to happen to every guy you love."

Stung, Nye blinked back the moisture that involuntarily sprang to her eyes. "You're right, Oriana. You don't understand. Just leave it at that, okay?"

Oriana crossed her arms and gazed out the passenger window.

In the brittle silence, Nye struggled to straighten out the mass of her tangled emotions. Yes, she did like Cullen. She had never been so attracted to any man since Dante's death, and the feeling terrified her. She had loved and lost—had her life smashed to pieces, nearly destroying her along with it. She would never let that happen again.

The only way she could guarantee there would be no more disasters was not to love in the first place. She had lived out that strategy for three years without much difficulty, and she could certainly continue to do so now. Or could she? A handsome face with the darkest brown eyes she had ever seen appeared in her mind and stayed there the rest of the way home.

Chapter Six

*"The dance which we dance is at the centre and
for the dance all things were made."*
–C. S. Lewis

*The two figures glide together, flowing in … out … in …
out, like the waves of the ocean they dance by. The woman's
blonde hair streaks out behind her in the strong ocean breeze
as the man spins her out and pulls her against him in one
graceful motion. He smiles at her, holds her close, for just a
moment. The warmth in his blue eyes fades, giving way to a
distant sadness. He drops his arms to his sides and backs
away. The woman's eyes widen as the man continues to back
toward the ocean. He stops, lifts his hand as if to reach for her,
then abruptly turns and walks into the water. The woman bolts
forward, frantically grasping, trying to stop him. He's always
out of reach, calmly walking into the ocean. The sky blackens.
The water soars to meet the storm. Angry waves rise to the sky
and crash before the man. Strands of soaked hair cling to the
woman's face, clutching at her eyes, blurring her vision. She
tries to follow. Water pushes against her legs. Her cold limbs
hang like lead. A wave shoots skyward and plunges, engulfing*

the man. She watches in horror. His hand slowly sinks into the ravaged ocean. "Dante!" Her anguished scream echoes, never ending.

Nye jolted awake and sat up in bed. Her heavy breathing was the only noise in the dark room.

Something cold touched her hand.

She jerked away.

It pressed her again, accompanied by a soft whine.

"Oh, Jordan." She bent over to rest her cheek on top of the dog's head as she stroked his fur. "I'm sorry, boy." She must have woken him. "It's okay." She looked at the clock. *3:32* glared at her in red numbers.

Rather than have another staring match with the clock for hours, Nye pushed off the covers and slipped her feet into soft slippers. The air in the house was chilly, and she stopped to pick up her fleece robe on the way out of the room. She walked to the kitchen, Jordan's padding following along behind her. She smiled despite her heavy heart. She didn't know what she would do without him. Wherever she went, he always seemed to be there, ready to comfort or support her if she needed it.

Nye poured coffee grounds and water into the coffeemaker and switched it on. The caffeine would likely keep her awake, but she needed something warm and strong—something to clear her head. She leaned her tired body against the counter. She hadn't had a nightmare that bad for several months and had taken that as a sign she was getting better.

Apparently, she had been wrong. All it took was an extended conversation with a charming man, and the dreams were back in full force. Of course, she reluctantly admitted, Cullen Chandler wasn't just any guy. He was a man who, for the first time in three years, had kept her from thinking about Dante for an hour.

That was why she had to make sure she didn't see Cullen any more than was necessary to do her job. She wasn't going to let herself get hurt again. Besides, Dante's memory was too strong to let her even consider allowing another man into her heart. At least, that had been the case until she met Cullen.

Nye pushed her hair back and let out a long breath. She had to rein in her winding thoughts.

So, Cullen was different. What should she do about it? Maybe it didn't matter. Maybe he had been scared off by her mother or Nye's own idiosyncrasies. If that were the case, they could then get through the Sheffield deal quickly and professionally with as little contact as possible. End of worries. For some reason, the thought wasn't as comforting as it should have been. Depression and a growing anxiousness were her companions as she sat at the table and drank her coffee, thinking about Dante and, despite her better judgment, Cullen.

Nye was nervous. She couldn't believe it. During her two years in this business, she had never once doubted her abilities or had an attack of nerves during a meeting. Yet here she was at the second conference with Sheffield, Inc., experiencing all the classic symptoms of stage fright. Nye clasped her trembling hands together and hid them in her lap as Claude Van Vechten discussed employee benefits stipulations.

After her sleepless night, Nye had thought her only trouble at the meeting with Sheffield today would be staying awake. How could she have forgotten about Cullen's effect on her? Sleep was the farthest thing from her mind with her nerves tingling every time she caught his dark eyes looking her way.

Nye usually took the lead at negotiations like this, but today she was barely a participant. Every time she spoke, Cullen watched, and she felt something ridiculously akin to the self-consciousness of a sixth-grade crush. It made the situation more maddening that Cullen didn't seem to have any difficulty concentrating. He had already impressed Nye multiple times with his skill and preparedness. His approach to this deal demonstrated a caliber of legal representation that Nye wasn't used to encountering in Harper.

Such obvious adeptness sitting across from her, combined with the importance of this deal to her firm, would normally motivate Nye to be at the top of her game. And why shouldn't it now? Anger for her lack of control and ridiculous behavior rose within. That's enough of that. She was not interested in him, she didn't want a relationship. She was a business professional. With those reminders, Nye applied her well-conditioned self-control and looked up, determined to take the helm for the rest of these negotiations.

Her disobedient heart fluttered when her gaze collided with Cullen's.

A small smile crept onto his face as he watched her.

The test to her resolve was a bit too much, and Nye looked away, only to see everyone else staring at her. They were waiting for something. Her mind raced to remember what they had been talking about. No good. She hadn't been paying attention for quite a while. Heat rose from her neck up.

Van Vechten's disapproving gaze bored holes in her vulnerable psyche. "Well, Ms. Sanders?"

She swallowed her mortification and forced what she hoped looked like a confident smile. "I'm sorry, can you repeat the question?"

Nye wasn't just mad, she was furious. She glared at herself in the mirror before she thrust her hands under the ice-cold water pouring from the faucet. Alone in the unnecessarily glamorous public restroom at Sheffield, Nye wanted to scream or, at least, splash her face, but the frigid water would only wash off her makeup and not her humiliation.

She stared at her reflection, seeing a confident, successful businesswoman who had just made a public spectacle of herself in front of her peers. And why? A man had waltzed into her life, apparently with the one purpose of turning her world upside down.

Nye sighed and reached for a paper towel. That wasn't fair. It was her fault, not his. Cullen hadn't done anything. That was the trouble. Just his presence in the same room was enough to turn her brain to sludge. She was sure this unexpected weakness on her part was only temporary. It had to be purely physical—a strong chemical reaction of some sort that would fade as she got used to being around him. Even so, she didn't see any reason her theory had to be put to the test.

Somewhere between her attempts to cover her embarrassment and the close of the meeting, Nye had come up with a solution to her problem. She would simply approach Dan Akkerman and ask if Derek Morris could take her place for the remainder of the negotiations. As a promising associate manager, Derek had overseen a number of negotiations and had done very well. Nye was sure she could talk Dan into letting the younger associate handle this deal to give him more experience and greater responsibilities.

Nye brushed aside the cowardly feeling that threatened to quash her relief at the prospect of ending her emotional struggle. It wasn't escaping … exactly. More like seeking shelter while a storm passed by. Nothing wrong with that.

The door swung open and Renee entered. She rested a concerned gaze on Nye. "Are you feeling okay? You seemed a little out of it in there."

Nye tossed the paper towel in the garbage and forced a bright smile. "Sure. I'm just fine."

"Good."

Renee didn't know her well enough to see through the pretense.

"Some of us are going to Aces for lunch. Want to come?" Renee asked over her shoulder, as she headed for one of the stalls.

"Uh, I don't think so. I have to meet with a property owner."

"Okay. Well, you know you're always welcome to join us if you can fit in time for lunch." Renee's voice floated over the door of the stall as she closed it.

"Thanks." Nye stepped into the hallway before she could feel guilty for ducking another of Renee's invitations. Since Nye had entered the business field, she strictly adhered to the guideline of keeping her coworkers at arm's length. Though she treated them kindly, she never shared her personal problems and encouraged the same restraint from them. Better to miss out on potential friendships than to face the consequences of emotional attachments at some later date.

At the end of the hallway, Nye punched the button for the elevator and waited.

An occasional lunch with her associates might not be too harmful, but Nye worried that today she would have to spend the time fending off personal questions about her strange behavior at the meeting. She'd rather be alone and plan for the optimum moment to approach Dan about Derek taking over the negotiations.

"Going to lunch?"

Nye started at the sound of Cullen's voice.

He came up next to her. "Sorry. Didn't mean to startle you."

"You didn't," she lied, staring at the elevator doors as the telltale heat of returning embarrassment rushed to her face. She couldn't even bear to look at him after the spectacle she'd made of herself. She had hoped to leave without having to face anyone, especially Cullen. He must be thinking of her as completely incompetent and wondering how she ever lasted this long at her firm. Even worse, he might have figured out that he was the reason she had been so distracted. Nye nearly choked on the thought. An involuntary cough pushed its way up her throat, only increasing her abashment.

The elevator doors opened, and Nye had to quell her instinct to rush for the avenue of escape. An older man and a middle-aged woman moved to one side as Nye and Cullen stepped in.

"Parking garage?" Cullen glanced at Nye, as he reached for the panel of buttons.

She nodded.

He selected the lower level and turned to her. "I'm glad the meeting was only a morning one. It seemed long."

He had no idea how gross an understatement that was. This ride was taking forever, too. Whoever thought elevators were a good idea? This was the closest she had ever been to Cullen, and the proximity was having a dizzying effect on her senses. Annoyance flared at his power over her, and she tried to inconspicuously move farther into the corner.

"It'll be nice to get something to eat. I'm planning to go to Fontenello's. Feel like Italian?"

Her irritation vanished at the unexpected invitation. She raised a startled gaze to his face. Lunch? Just the two of them? Sheer panic raced through her veins, mixing with a feeling uncomfortably close to excitement. "Um … thanks, but …" Her mind went blank. Again. What had her excuse been?

The elevator slowed to a halt, and the two other passengers disembarked.

Nye watched them exit, hoping she would just look distracted, as she floundered in her panicked jumble of thoughts. Of course—Russell Flanagan. "I'm going straight to another business meeting." She barely hid her relief at remembering the iron-clad excuse as the doors closed and the elevator carried them downward.

"No break for lunch?"

"I might eat on the way. It's quite a drive."

"Sounds like they work you pretty hard."

She met his gaze and tried to ignore the warmth that surged through her at the sight of those dark eyes. "I'm sure you know what that's like, being a lawyer."

"You could say that."

Was that a hint of disappointment behind Cullen's gentle smile? Nye looked away, dismissing the thought. The invitation had been casual enough—completely appropriate for business associates who represented opposite sides in contract negotiations. Any serious intentions on his part would be unethical in a legal sense. Then why did her pulse still feel like it was training for a marathon?

The doors opened, and Nye stepped through, avoiding the answer to that question.

"Have a nice afternoon."

"You, too." Nye didn't look back as she hurried to her car, more convinced than ever that she had to get out of working on this deal, and that she had to stay away from Cullen Chandler.

Cullen ran a hand through his hair as he watched Nye rush to her car. On Sunday, he thought he had started to break through her walls. She had begun to relax and even seemed to enjoy their conversation. But today, it was like they were back to square one with Nye carefully keeping him at a distance— that is, when she wasn't dashing away as if afraid he was going to catch her. Her unpredictable behavior left him more than a little frustrated.

He shook his head and headed for his car, his thoughts turning to the many tasks waiting for him at the office. He didn't really have time for lunch anyway. Skipping it was probably a good idea. He pressed the button on his remote to unlock the car door, just as his cell phone vibrated. He pulled it out of his pocket and glanced at the caller ID as he slid into the car. "Hi, Mom."

"Hi, honey. How are you?"

"Okay. You?"

"Couldn't be better. Are you on your lunch break?"

"Of course." He frowned at the insecurity in his mother's voice. She often called during his break, but she was always afraid she was interrupting his work. "Your timing is impeccable." Especially since her call gave him a respite from his confused thoughts about Nye.

"Well, thank you. Are you eating right now?"

"No, not yet." He could picture his mom working in the kitchen as she talked. For years, Monday had been the day when she concocted the wonderful creations that had delighted Cullen and his brother, as well as their fortunate neighbors and people from church. Cullen smiled, almost able to smell the aroma of fresh-baked cookies.

"I'll make this short so you can eat."

He started the engine and checked over his shoulder before backing out of the stall. "No rush. I'm just driving." He wasn't about to tell her that he had decided to forego lunch. His mother was wonderful about trying not to meddle in his life, but he didn't want to test her limits.

"I'm calling about your granddad."

"What about him?" Cullen tensed, not liking the concerned note in her words. He stopped the car at the exit and handed the attendant his parking voucher.

"I just wondered how he's doing."

"Oh." Relieved she hadn't been about to break bad news, Cullen looked both directions and pulled onto the street. "Fine, I think. Why?"

"I talked to him on the phone yesterday, and I thought he sounded a little ... odd."

"What do you mean, 'odd'?"

"I don't know, really. Not quite himself. Like he wasn't telling me something."

"Maybe he was just tired," Cullen offered, trying to calm the anxiety he heard in her voice. His mother was smart and level-headed, but she had always been quick to worry and overreact to anything abnormal, especially concerning her loved ones.

"I know. I'm probably worrying over nothing."

He was surprised to hear her admit it.

"But I thought you could set my mind at rest. Have you seen him recently?"

Cullen swallowed the guilty feeling that arose with her question. "No, not recently. I've wanted to get out there. Work has just been so crazy."

"Oh."

He signaled for a turn, thankful for something to do during the awkward pause.

"Well, I know you're doing your best. I'm sure he's fine. Anyway, I know it isn't anything serious." Her tone changed with an apparent decision to sound more positive.

"I'll try to visit him as soon as I can. Maybe tomorrow. Okay?"

"That'd be nice, but don't do it for my sake. I know your firm works you so hard already. I don't mean to add any pressure."

Every word she said added to his guilt, but it was innocently done. "I know you don't. I really want to see him. It just hasn't worked out lately."

"I understand. I can tell you're busy, so I better let you go. Talk to you soon."

"Okay. Love you."

"Love you, too. Bye-bye, sweetie."

Cullen let out a grunt of frustration as he ended the call. How was he supposed to do it all? It wasn't his fault that doing a good job at the firm meant putting in so many hours. He had a responsibility to do his best there, to perform to the standards required. He had to succeed. At Venning, success meant sacrifice. He just wished his family and friends didn't have to be among those sacrifices. Maybe he needed to try harder. If he pushed himself more, maybe he could fit in the people he had been forced to neglect.

He glanced at the clock. It was too late in the lunch hour to visit his grandfather now. By the time he drove out to the ranch, he'd have to turn around and head right back to work. But the conversation with his mom left Cullen unsettled, almost fidgety. He needed to do something. He thought of the other relationships that had suffered because of his job.

Grant. Cullen had lately turned down all of his friend's countless invitations to play tennis or get together during the week.

Cullen changed lanes, heading for a different destination. He was close to the tennis club, and Grant would be only a block away at his office. If Cullen called Grant now, they could squeeze in a few sets. Cullen only hoped seeing his friend and working off some steam would assuage the guilt he couldn't seem to shake.

Chapter Seven

"How can we know the dancer from the dance?"
–William Butler Yeats

"Mr. Flanagan?" Nye cautiously approached Russell, who sat on a porch bench near his front door and stared at the white expanse of snow.

He turned his head to her, his eyes blank and distant.

"Are you all right?" Her pulse sped up, as she mentally ran through the little she knew about symptoms of a heart attack.

He blinked, and his gaze cleared. "Oh, hello there. I was just thinking … remembering." His eyes twinkled. "At my age, that takes a lot of doing. Can't expect me to do two things at once anymore."

"Aren't you cold?" He wore a jacket this time, but she still didn't think it was good for such an elderly man to sit outside in the winter air.

He shook his head. "Grew up in this weather."

So had Nye, but that didn't make her immune to the cold. She tried to keep the thought to herself, but Russell took one look at her and unnervingly read her like a book.

"People have different constitutions, I reckon. Maybe it's the memories that keep me warm." He looked out across the powdered land. "Used to be a big pasture right out there." He gestured to the land on the right of the driveway. "Right there's where I taught Gloria to ride. My grandsons, too."

"You have grandchildren?" Nye had guessed as much from the photos she had seen, but it never hurt to encourage conversation with a property owner. At least, that's what she told herself she was doing, even as she felt more genuine interest in his answer than she ordinarily would have with a business contact.

"Yep. Two grandsons. My daughter's children." His voice held deep pride.

"Do you see them much?"

"They're grown men now. They have their own lives to live."

Nye pushed her hands into her coat pockets. He reached for his crutches. "We best get you inside."

Nye couldn't help the smile that touched her lips at his grandfatherly concern. He stood and held the door for her.

"Coffee's in there." He nodded to the living room she had peeked into during her last visit. "Go on in and have a seat." He took off his cap and hung it on the coat rack as she followed his directions.

The old fashioned comfort of the living room covered her like a warm blanket, inviting her to a much-needed respite from the emotional battle that had raged during her drive out of the city. Though the delicate doilies and collectibles that filled nooks and crannies didn't suit Nye's taste, they added sweetness to the setting, softening the dark tones of the elegant wooden tables and bookcases that were so surprising in this humble man's house.

Nye sank onto the worn sofa and determined to clear her mind of the Cullen dilemma. She took a deep breath and noticed the wooden chess set that was assembled on the polished surface of the coffee table in front of her. The beautiful, intricately carved pieces and board looked like collector's items that must have cost a great deal. The contract she had given Russell lay near the chess set, between two steaming mugs of the promised beverage. What had Russell decided about the offer? She started to prepare herself for his potential concerns.

Russell entered the room on his crutches, his white hair smoothed as if it had just been combed. "I'm afraid the answer's not what you want to hear."

Nye blinked. How did he do that? Despite his harmless appearance, this elderly man's ability to read her thoughts made him dangerous. What other things that she tried so hard to cover could he see? Brushing aside the disturbing question, she focused on business.

"You weren't happy with the offer?" She took a sip of coffee, hoping the energy boost would return her to normal—unreadable and detached.

He headed for the large armchair across from her. "Parts of it were all right." He lowered himself into the chair and leaned his crutches against the armrest.

"Which aspects don't you like?" She leaned forward and set her mug on the table.

He watched her with a sharp gaze. "It's not what's in there. You're offering a fair price, like you say. It's more what's not in there that worries me."

"What do you mean?"

"Casinos." He pressed his lips into a hard line. "Those other fellows all wanted to build casinos on my land. I won't allow that."

"What don't you like about casinos?" She could guess, but she wanted to be sure.

"The Good Book says the Lord is against gambling, and I've seen the damage it does to folks. That contract you gave me doesn't say anything about who your buyers are. I want to make sure they aren't casino men."

Nye took a moment to think about her response. She had never encountered a religious obstacle to closing a sale before. It presented an unusual challenge. She took a breath. She was treading on thin ice. "We don't actually know at this point, for certain, who our buyer will be." Despite the tug she felt on her conscience, she decided not to admit that their current target buyer was a casino owner who wanted to construct another gaming center on the Flanagan property.

"Can you guarantee me you won't sell the land for a casino?"

"Mr. Flanagan," she met his gaze, "it's enormously difficult for us to regulate what buyers do with a property once it's in their possession. The land belongs to them at that point, and they can do as they see fit." Technically, her statements were true. Why, then, was she questioning her methods? She ignored her conscience to make one last pitch. "And we can only offer you such a good price when we're free, as you are, to pursue the most lucrative offer presented to us."

"I'd take less money if I could get it put in the contract nobody can build casinos here." Russell set his mug on a round table by the chair. He grabbed his crutches and stood, looking at her with a serious gaze. "I like your offer best so far. You get that put in, and I'll take another look. But no casino's going to be built on my land."

Nye took in the determined set of his jaw and the flash at the back of his eyes. He wasn't going to budge. She nodded and rose from the sofa. "All right, Mr. Flanagan. I'll look into having that stipulation put into the contract. I don't know that I'll be able to get it for you, but I'll try."

His eyes softened, and his shoulders visibly relaxed. "That's good enough for me. Thank you."

"No, thank you." She smiled, but her mind was already working on the problem in front of her. She didn't think it likely that any of the principals at KBA would agree to cut out their highest bidder among the potential buyers. But if they couldn't even purchase Russell's land because of his demands, KBA would lose out on a profitable sale.

Nye tried to convince herself that the financial loss to her firm was the only reason she cared so much about making this deal work. She told herself it had nothing to do with the tender concern that grew inside her as she shook his hand, feeling his stiff fingers, the vulnerability of his age. She couldn't afford to care for anyone. Not even a kind, elderly man who saw so much more than she wanted him to and made her wonder what he knew about this life that she didn't.

Cullen swung his racket at the ball, hitting nothing but air.

"That's game!" Grant Walker jogged to the net with a grin.

Cullen waved his hand to acknowledge Grant's victory. "Nice point." Cullen wiped sweat off his forehead.

Grant walked to Cullen's side of the tennis court. "What can I say? God-given talent." He posed with the racquet as if about to release a whopping backhand swing.

Cullen shook his head, smiling at his friend's antics.

Grant's joking expression transitioned to a thoughtful one.

"You doing all right?"

Cullen shrugged and went to the bench where they had left their water bottles. He took a slow drink, buying time to formulate an answer. He had long ago gotten used to Grant's blunt manner and rapid mood changes. But even having anticipated such a question hadn't given Cullen a ready answer. He didn't know where to start. Nye? Work? Knowing how Grant felt about Cullen's approach to his job, he guessed it'd be safer sticking to his emotional troubles.

"You take any longer to drink that water, and I'm going to call the paramedics."

Cullen set the bottle down with another smile.

Grant collapsed onto the bench. "Look, if you don't want to talk about it, that's fine, but something's got you seriously distracted. You usually kill—" He grinned. "I mean, tend to do better than me on the court."

"You're right." Cullen sat on the bench and glanced at his friend. "About both."

"Ouch." Grant took a swig from his water bottle.

Cullen sucked in a deep breath. "Do you know Nye Sanders at all?"

Grant squinted. "Sanders? Oh, isn't she related to Marcus and Caroline Sanders from church?"

Cullen nodded. "Their daughter."

"That's right. I remember hearing about her. Blonde and beautiful, right? No wonder you're distracted."

Cullen stared pensively at the court.

"I'm assuming she's the problem?"

"Oh, yeah." Cullen leaned forward and ran his hands down his face. "She's representing a PE firm in a deal I'm working on. I don't know what's wrong with me." He looked at Grant. "I've never felt like this about anyone. I can't concentrate when she's around. Can't stop thinking about her when she isn't. I dream about her ... I ..." He trailed off with a sigh and reached in his duffel bag for a towel.

Grant twirled his racket. "Do you know how she feels?"

"That's the really confusing part." Cullen wiped sweat off his neck with the towel. "The first times we spoke, she was friendly, interested. I even thought she might ... you know ... feel the same way."

"But?"

"She's almost cold now, and I can't shake the feeling that she's purposefully avoiding me."

"Doesn't sound too promising."

Trust Grant to knock aside the positive guff Cullen had been feeding himself and dump a cold dose of reality. Cullen sighed. "You're right. Normally I'd back off and leave her alone, but ... there's this sadness in her eyes. Something's pulling her under. Something awful. I don't know what, but she's hurting, and I ..."

"You want to help." Grant leaned forward. "A couple years back, I heard something about a tragedy. Something happened with Nye or someone she knew. I don't know the details, but the whole family always seems really concerned about her." Grant turned to Cullen with a probing gaze. "I know you want to help her, but … are you sure you have time for that kind of relationship?"

Cullen looked away. They hadn't spoken of their disagreement over the phone, both silently agreeing to ride it out without another confrontation. At least, that was what Cullen hoped. He hadn't expected Grant to throw the situation in his face.

Grant blew out a long breath. "Look, man, I'm sorry. You don't have to be accountable to me for when you talk to your grandfather." He blew out a breath. "I just … you call me up to play twenty minutes of tennis on your lunch break, during which you didn't even eat. Something's off, you know?"

Cullen stared blankly at the empty court. "Yeah."

"That's why I can't help but wonder if this thing with Nye is going to be too much. I mean, can you really handle anything more right now?"

Cullen couldn't deny Grant had a point. Yet the image of Nye's beautiful, sad gaze stuck with Cullen like a shadow, making his heart ache. He couldn't dismiss the possibility of a relationship with her—not before he even had a chance. He faced his friend. "I keep remembering those first times I talked to her. I don't know if she meant to or not, but something in her eyes pleaded for help. And if you could've seen her when she finally smiled, and the haunted look went away …"

"Yep, you're a goner." Grant smiled and leaned back on the bench, lacing his hands behind his head. "Okay, pal. Maybe you should see how she feels. Why don't you ask her to lunch or something?"

Cullen winced. "Tried that."

"Bide your time. Be patient. Pray about it. If it's meant to happen, God will show you the right moment to try again. Then you'll find out where you stand. And then we can get a real game of tennis out of you."

Cullen threw the towel at his grinning friend. His stomach curdled with excitement. Maybe Grant's idea wasn't so bad. At least Cullen could get closer to discovering Nye's true feelings. Maybe it would finally put an end to his heart's state of limbo. On the other hand, what if she said no again?

Cullen hoisted the duffel bag to his shoulder and followed Grant to the locker rooms. He would leave that question for God to answer. After all, God had brought Nye into Cullen's life for a reason, and even his jumbled feelings for her were safely in the hands of the Creator.

Having made her pitch to Dan regarding Mr. Flanagan's property, Nye stood in front of his desk awaiting Dan's answer.

"Absolutely not."

She blinked. What? Dan's laissez-faire approach to

business usually meant he easily acquiesced, not caring enough to have an opinion. She knew any of the other KBA principals would oppose a move that would obstruct the most profitable sale possibility, but she hoped Dan would be an exception. No such luck. He might be hands-off, but he wasn't stupid.

He folded his arms across his chest and leaned back in the desk chair. Sunlight from the window behind him glinted off his sand-colored hair, which was beginning to prematurely gray.

"Mr. Akkerman—"

"Dan." His eyes twinkled as he made the automatic correction. "And will you please sit down?"

Nye stifled the urge to roll her eyes as she sat in the chair facing the desk. She didn't like to encourage the name game they had played since her arrival at the firm. After she had rebuffed his initial attempts to have more than a professional relationship, Dan continued to drop hints that he was still interested. She insisted on calling him by his last name, using the formality to make her boundaries clear. There was nothing discomfiting about Dan's pursuit of her, so she tolerated his suggestions as the good-natured teasing they were intended to be.

"Mr. Akkerman," she continued, "if we don't respect Mr. Flanagan's wishes in this case, he refuses to sell to us at all. I believe if we compromise on this point and agree not to sell to anyone who will build a casino on the land, we can purchase the property and still make a substantial profit."

"By selling to whom?"

"There were two interested parties who intended to use the land for a shopping mall."

A shrewd awareness appeared behind the innocence of his curious gaze. "And their offers were less than the casino reps', right?"

She wished she could deny it. "Not a great deal, but less would be better than nothing."

"Nothing." He narrowed his eyes, but a smile played on his lips. "You're telling me you can't talk a penniless, lonely old geezer into selling his land?"

She steadily met his gaze. "He's not a 'geezer,' and it's harder than you might think. He has very strong convictions about it. It has to do with his faith."

"Right. Nye, you could convince me to jump off Big Ben with one smile. What's the problem? His lawyer can't be going along with this. It'll mean less money."

She swallowed. "He doesn't have a lawyer."

Dan blinked at her. "You're kidding."

She didn't like the ruthless glint in his eyes as he smiled.

"That's no match for you, Nye. You'll get him to sign the contract the way it is."

She didn't know what to say as her conscience battled

with her business sense and habitual adherence to the decisions
made by her superiors.

"Now that we have that settled, I want to hear about the
Harrison sale," he said, mentioning the name of the portfolio
company she was trying to sell to Sheffield. "Is Sheffield ready
to close?"

The swiftness of the subject change caught her off-guard.
With the bitter taste of defeat in her mouth, she would have
chosen to wait for a more opportune moment to broach her
other request, but when she visualized another meeting with
Cullen, panic spurred her onward. "No, they want more
changes made to the offer, but I actually wanted to talk to you
about that."

"Oh?"

"The negotiations are improving, and I'm getting so busy
with other projects, that we might want to let Derek take over."

"You mean take you off the deal?" Dan stared at her,
eyebrows raised.

"Yes." She flinched, startled by the strength of his
reaction. She could understand his financial reasoning in the
Flanagan case, but why did he care about this? "It would be a
wonderful opportunity for Derek. And for the firm, of course.
It's a good chance to see what he can do with a bigger sale."
Nye watched his unchanging expression and began to question
her decision to talk about this now. Maybe she'd been too
hasty, and should have waited until a different time. If she

wasn't so anxious at the thought of more meetings with Cullen, she might have given herself more time to plan her method of attack.

Too late to turn back now. She had to convince Dan. "I should have suggested Derek for this deal right away, but I just didn't think of it when you first gave me the file. If you're worried about him being ready, I can vouch he's more than—"

He held up his hand. "Look, Nye." He stood and rounded the desk. He perched on the edge, sitting in front of her to meet her gaze. "This deal is extremely important to our firm. As the principal overseeing the negotiations, I'm responsible for their success or failure. I know you think Derek is ready, and he probably is."

She opened her mouth to respond.

"But," Dan lifted his finger, "I can't risk this deal. It's too big. With you, there are no doubts. I know you'll deliver."

"That's very nice of you but—"

He stood and looked down at her, uncharacteristically serious. "I don't want to argue with you, Nye. I need you on this deal, and I need you to handle it quickly. With dispatch. Okay?" The finality in the question strongly indicated what her answer should be.

She was in danger of pushing too far. He had no reason to understand her need to get away from this deal, and she couldn't explain it to him. With a sinking feeling in her stomach, she nodded. "If you think it's best."

"I do." He went back to his swivel desk chair and sat down, turning to face her with his usual teasing grin restored. "Well, that was easy. Now if only I could get you to say yes to dinner that quickly, I'd be in business."

She shook her head and rose to leave. "How's Monica?" she asked, referring to his on-again, off-again girlfriend.

He dismissed the reminder with a wave of his hand. "Eh, she wouldn't mind."

"Right." Nye exited and closed the door behind her. The sight of Rachel, Dan's secretary, was the only thing that kept Nye from slumping against the door. The defeat of her escape plan from the Sheffield deal brought Nye's fatigue washing over her in a sudden flood.

She summoned her strength and passed Rachel at the desk with what she hoped would appear to be a normal expression. A short distance down the hallway, Nye reached her office and gratefully entered the private sanctuary. She walked to the window to close the blinds.

She paused, her gaze irresistibly drawn to the State Bank building. The skyscraper loomed above the surrounding structures as if boasting of its status as the tallest building in Harper. Which floor housed Cullen's office? Could he see her from there?

Nye jerked away from the window, shocked at her wayward train of thought. She sat behind the desk. She was exhausted. She wasn't herself.

The attempt at excuses did little to reassure her. She was tired, but her fatigue was caused by nightmares that resulted from Cullen being in her life. Thanks to her job, that situation was not going to change anytime soon. She would have to find a way to shut down her reaction to him and focus on getting through the negotiations. It shouldn't be that difficult. She had quickly killed any sparks of interest she might have had for any man since Dante's death, but she wasn't going to pretend Cullen would be as easy to dismiss. After a morning's struggle with her reaction to him, she knew better.

Squelching her attraction to him would require great effort, but nothing would ever demand as much strength as the circumstances she had already survived. Memories of the nightmare from the evening before flickered in her mind, and the familiar, icy ache clamped around her heart. How strange. She hadn't realized until now that the awful feeling had left her for a time. At least the internal struggle triggered by Cullen's presence had that benefit. But it was only temporary. Feelings like those she had for Cullen would ultimately bring more pain. They couldn't make the ache stay away. They couldn't heal. They couldn't bring Dante back. Nothing could.

She clenched her jaw with the anger that grew out of the coldness in her chest. God had tried to beat her down before, and she had survived. She could certainly get over a little crush.

She stood and reached for the cord that controlled the

blinds. She would get over it. She yanked the cord, and the blinds covered the window with a satisfying snap.

Chapter Eight

"The Great Dance does not wait to be perfect until the peoples of the Low Worlds are gathered into it. We speak not of when it will begin. It has begun from before always."
–C. S. Lewis

Cullen proofed the document in front of him, trying hard to concentrate.

"Night, Cullen." Rhonda Greerson leaned into Cullen's office and waved.

Cullen glanced up from his desk. "Going home?"

"Yep." The associate lawyer looked as exhausted as Cullen felt. "Have any plans for tonight?"

He looked at the clock. "To get out of here in twenty minutes?"

She laughed. "That's the spirit. Good luck. Oh …" She lowered her voice. "Blanchard's still here."

"Thanks."

As soon as Rhonda left, Cullen leaned forward in his chair, pushing to finish the document on his computer screen as quickly as he could. This revision of the purchase agreement should mark the completion of one of the many deals on his plate. If he managed to finish it in the time he quoted to

Rhonda, he would even be able to surprise his grandfather with a visit. It was a weeknight, but his grandfather had said to stop in anytime.

Cullen was determined to resolve at least one of the problems that had been hounding him all week. Seeing Nye at several more Sheffield meetings and resisting the urge to talk to her, other than as a lawyer, had been far more difficult than he anticipated. He tried to give her space, to wait and see what happened as Grant advised. But nothing changed. Nye still disappeared as soon as each session ended, never approaching him to talk as he had hoped. In desperate need of guidance, Cullen continued to pray about his feelings for her, but God responded by strengthening those emotions. At least, Cullen hoped he was heeding God and not merely his own desires.

On top of his confusion with Nye, Cullen had been trying unsuccessfully to squeeze in a visit to his grandfather. The unsettled feeling that had started during Cullen's conversation with his mother hadn't dissipated. Grant might be right—there probably was something wrong with the way work had taken over Cullen's world. But at the same time, he didn't see any other option. At least tonight, God had opened up an opportunity for Cullen to fix things with his grandfather. Cullen still had many projects he should work on, of course, but he was finishing the most urgent one now. The other cases had less pressing deadlines, and he was determined they wouldn't stop him from fitting in the long-overdue visit.

He finally breathed as he finished reviewing the last paragraph. It was done. He slid his chair back and looked at the phone, wondering if he should call his grandfather to warn him. He reached for the receiver and jumped as the phone rang under his hand.

He picked it up. "Yes?"

"Chandler."

Cullen would recognize Blanchard's tight, nasal voice anywhere.

"I need to see you in my office."

"Now?"

Silence.

"I'll be right there." Cullen replaced the receiver, dread sinking to the pit of his stomach. A summons to Blanchard's office was never a good thing. He glanced at the clock as he stood, hoping Blanchard wouldn't take long. Cullen hated his helpless feeling as he entered the dim hallway and headed for the shaft of light shining from the partner's office. He certainly couldn't tell Blanchard that he needed to go. Leaving the office at eight o'clock was the mark of a slacker by Blanchard's autocratic standards. Nevertheless, Cullen refused to be intimidated by anyone. If bullying was what Blanchard had in mind, he would have to find a different victim.

Cullen reached the door of the office and knocked.

"Come in."

Cullen entered and strode confidently toward the desk, watching the top of Blanchard's head as he bent over his work. Cullen risked an impatient clearing of his throat.

Blanchard looked up. "Did you finish the Emerson agreement yet?"

"Yes."

"Good." A glimmer of approval appeared in Blanchard's eyes then vanished. His mouth thinned into a hard line. "I understand you haven't made much progress on the Sheffield deal."

"With all due respect, sir, that isn't true."

Blanchard's lips curled. "Isn't it?"

"No, we've made quite a bit of progress. We're—"

"When will the deal close?"

"I can't say for sure at this point, but it's looking good."

Blanchard's eyes narrowed as he frowned.

Cullen grappled for a date, some reasonable time frame that would at once please his boss and not be unreachable. "Another week should bring us very close." A week? What if that was true? Could he really say good-bye to Nye that soon? His heart plummeted as he momentarily forgot the cantankerous man who glared at him.

"We expect more from a lawyer with your credentials, Chandler."

Blanchard's scolding tone brought Cullen back to the problem in from of him.

"The Sheffield deal is now your primary focus. Put in more hours if necessary. Whatever it takes. Understood?"

Cullen nodded, but the gesture was lost on Blanchard, who had already returned to reviewing the papers in front of him. Cullen turned on his heels and left the office, his frustration threatening to explode into anger. While it would be enormously satisfying to blow up at Blanchard, an outburst would also destroy all chances of partnership or even job security—the goals that drove Cullen to keep up this lifestyle in the first place. He was quite sure the Lord wouldn't be too happy with what he'd like to say to Blanchard, either.

Cullen entered his office and took some deep breaths, trying to calm his temper. He searched through a stack of folders and found the Sheffield documents halfway down the pile. Sinking into his chair, he opened the file in the only clear space of his desk.

He gazed at the picture of his grandfather. With Cullen's pride in his work ethic still smarting from Blanchard's accusations, leaving early tonight was out of the question. Cullen hoped the grandfather who had been such a gentle, wise influence in his youth, would understand. The visit would have to wait.

Nye exited the conference room at Sheffield, Inc., with her old confidence safely locked in place. This week of negotiations was going much more to her liking. Since her embarrassing showing at the second meeting, Nye had worked to repair the damage done to her reputation by taking control of the deal and representing her firm with the skill that earned her paycheck. She had been able to accelerate the negotiation process, and the deal showed signs of heading for a close.

As for coping with Cullen, she had found success with a new method—pretending he wasn't there. It sounded juvenile, even to Nye, but it worked. Using a technique she had learned years ago for calming performance anxiety, she manipulated her mental vision of the audience at these meetings until, at least in her mind, Cullen was no longer there. She still had to deal with an occasional flutter in her stomach—a reaction that refused to submit to her will—when she caught Cullen watching her or when she relaxed too much and found herself contemplating his smile. Fortunately, such lapses in her focus were few.

As another precaution, she left the building as quickly as possible when the meetings adjourned. She spotted Cullen observing her quick escapes on a few occasions, but tried to act like she hadn't seen him. An annoying feeling of cowardice cloaked her successful exits whenever she felt his gaze on her. She had to admit it might be gutless to avoid him, maybe even rude. Yet she didn't dare let him get close to her, talk to her, or pin her under that gaze. She might be able to resist him at a distance, but she didn't want to try a close-range test.

With that caution in mind, Nye surreptitiously checked for Cullen as she headed for the elevators. The meeting had let out for the day, and Nye ducked out of the conference room before Cullen. She didn't see him now, but she wasn't about to turn around to be sure.

She sighed as the elevator doors closed at the end of the hall. That meant extra walking for her. As part of her getaway plan, she now took the stairs instead of waiting if the elevator was delayed.

She reached the door to the staircase, resisting the temptation to check behind her. No need to look as if she was trying to escape. She pushed through the heavy door and started down the cement steps.

The door clanged shut behind her, echoing in the cavernous stairwell.

She heard it open again. She paused, wondering who had followed. Unable to resist, she looked back. Her heart lurched at the sight of Cullen standing at the top of the staircase. How could anyone look that good under fluorescent lighting?

He watched her with a question in his gaze. "Getting your exercise?"

She smiled shakily as that blasted fluttering sensation returned. "I guess." She turned to continue down the stairs.

He easily made up the distance between them and walked beside her.

So much for her great escape.

"I wanted to talk to you about the Harrison Company."

"Oh?" She glanced at him in surprise. He followed her to talk about business? She should be relieved. Instead, she found herself swallowing a feeling of disappointment. At least his professional demeanor was less difficult to resist than the charming grin he used to bestow on her. Then why did she miss that disarming feature?

"I was looking at the company's accounts, and there are a few points, possible discrepancies actually, that I'd like to go over with you. Maybe we could discuss them over lunch?"

"Oh, well, I ..." She grappled for an excuse. Difficult to find one when he was only suggesting a business meeting.

"You do have to eat, right?"

Something in his tone made her look at him.

There was a teasing twinkle in his eyes as he stopped walking and turned toward her.

She paused, pulse surging at a world record pace under his steady gaze.

Then he did it. His mouth spread into that ice-melting smile. "Think of it as multi-tasking."

Before she knew what she was doing, the word "Okay" slipped out.

"Great!" There was no missing the enthusiasm in his voice as he turned away and headed down the steps.

Nye snapped out of her daze and realized she was frozen on the stairs. She rushed to keep up with his brisk pace, searching through the confused muddle of her mind to figure out how she had let herself say yes.

"Where do you want to eat?"

"I was going to the cafeteria," she blurted. The noisy and crowded atmosphere would provide the perfect, non-romantic setting she needed.

"The cafeteria?" He looked playfully appalled. "You must've never eaten there."

She swallowed, trying to find her voice. "I don't have much time to go anywhere else."

"We'll find something close. How about Mario's? I like Italian cuisine, in case you can't tell." He flashed that grin again, and she was putty in his hands.

"Sure," she found herself breathing the word before she could come to her senses. She gulped as she followed him out the door to the parking garage. This promised to be the longest lunch hour of her life.

Chapter Nine

"We played the flute for you,
And you did not dance;
We mourned to you,
And you did not weep."
–Luke 7:32

By the time they were seated at the restaurant, Nye had formulated a new survival plan. Stick to business and get through the meal as quickly as possible. Now she had to make sure her rebellious emotions and the charming man across from her cooperated.

Setting her jaw with determination, she met Cullen's gaze. "You mentioned some discrepancies?"

He met her question with a smile and pointed to the menu in front of her. "We're supposed to eat, too, remember?" He lifted his menu. "Unless you already know what you're going to have?"

"Oh. No." She opened her menu, resisting the desire to hide her heated face behind it. She refused to become flustered again. Refocusing on speed as her goal, she tried to pick quickly from the menu options.

She looked at Cullen. "Do you come here often?"

"I've been here a few times."

"Any recommendations?"

"The baked ziti is fantastic."

"Sounds good." She closed the menu and set it aside. "That's what I'll have."

As if on cue, a young man approached to take their order. Nye felt Cullen's gaze as she ordered, and she tried to shake the unfamiliar self-consciousness that resulted.

As the server left, Nye turned to Cullen, about to bring up the purpose of their meeting.

"I saw your family again at church on Sunday," he said, before she could open her mouth.

She tensed. What had they told him about her?

"They're really great."

"Yes … they are."

He flashed a grin. "I hear you're a wickedly good Scrabble player."

She breathed again and returned his smile. "I haven't played for a very long time."

"I play a mean game myself. Maybe I can convince you to dust off your skills and take me on sometime."

To her surprise, she actually laughed. "I don't know. I'm not sure I'd be up to the challenge."

His grin broadened. "I'll go easy on you."

A tingle ran up her spine at the gleam in his eyes. She cleared her suddenly dry throat. "When was the last time you played?"

"Oh, wow. A long time." He leaned back and glanced at the ceiling. "The last time was with my grandfather, I think."

"That's right. You mentioned he lives here?"

Cullen met her gaze. "Yeah, just outside Harper. He's the one who taught me how to play Scrabble, actually. Taught me a lot of things." He stared at the candle between them, apparently lost in a memory. He suddenly looked up with a smile. "Chess was our big thing, though. We loved chess. Used to play a game every day when I stayed with him."

Despite her better judgment, Nye felt a growing curiosity. She was intrigued by the image of Cullen as a boy. "Did you do that often? Stay with your grandparents?"

"Every summer from the time I was twelve." His eyes darkened as he became more serious. "My brother got into some trouble around that time, and my parents thought it'd be a good idea for him to get away from bad influences. It was a wonderful move on their part. Granddad really straightened Chase out." A smile played on his lips. "Chase is a pastor now."

"Really?" She barely masked her chagrin. His brother was a pastor? The chasm between them widen.

"Now that you found out more about me, it's my turn."

She swallowed.

"I've been curious. How'd you get into private equity?"

"The same as anyone, I suppose. After I got my MBA, I applied for the first good job opening in Harper." She shrugged. "I got the position, and the rest is history."

"Do you enjoy it?"

"It's a good job." She fought the urge to squirm under his interested gaze. Somehow, her normal evasive answer to that question didn't feel right. She took a breath. "No, I don't really enjoy the work. It pays well. Provides security. That's enough for me."

He nodded, seeming to understand.

Why was she being so open? She wasn't even that honest with her family about her lack of interest in the job. It must be his laid back, relaxed demeanor. With one question, he was getting her to openly discuss things she didn't speak of with anyone. If she wasn't careful, she would end up telling him much more than was safe. Even so, the warning bells that pealed in her head were muffled under the warmth of his gaze. If she knew what was good for her, she would shift the focus of the conversation, fast. "Do you like being a lawyer?"

He winced. "Touché." He crossed his arms. "Yes and no, I guess. The workload is ridiculous. I don't like that, but I do enjoy the nature of the work itself. It's interesting."

Before she could comment, he turned the tables on her again.

"What about dance? Did you like that better?"

The question slammed into the face of Nye's curiosity. She froze. Like it? Dancing was like breathing, a passion that had been her life until she had met Dante, and the two loves converged into one. She couldn't explain to Cullen what it was like when her greatest love became her greatest pain—when breathing hurt.

"You said you majored in dance." Cullen glanced down and smoothed the tablecloth with his hand.

She tried to breathe through her rising panic.

"It doesn't really seem to go with business. Did you dance professionally at all?"

She managed a stiff nod, her throat constricting. This is what she got for letting her guard down. She had allowed his charm to lull her into a feeling of safety that made her want to be honest and open, a position that left her vulnerable to this blindsided attack.

"What kind of dancing did you do?"

"Tango." She was shocked at the normal sound of her voice.

"Wow." He leaned forward with a curious light in his eyes. "Why did you quit?"

With impeccable timing, the waiter approached the table with their drinks. He placed a glass of water in front of her, a natural interruption that bought her time.

She grasped the glass like a lifeline, willing her hand to stop shaking. The cool liquid ran down her throat as she drank, hoping the chill would jolt her into regaining control.

She set the glass down and looked at him with a calm façade. She even managed a placid smile, though she couldn't quite meet his gaze. "Shouldn't we talk about those discrepancies now?"

Cullen watched Nye, strangely fascinated. There it was again. That distanced, unreadable expression cloaked her eyes, creating a wall designed to shut him out.

He slowly leaned back in his chair. "Sure, if you'd like." It was the dancing topic again. What was she avoiding? Or was she hiding something? His mind raced to find an answer as he prepared to delve into his excuse for this meeting.

Initially, guilt had pricked at him for concocting a business reason to get her to come. Not that what he said wasn't true. There were some points related to the Harrison Company that needed to be clarified. He just hadn't mentioned that he probably could have resolved the issues himself with a little more digging.

When he looked across the table at those blue eyes, he didn't care how he had gotten her there. He had tried to take advantage of this opportunity to know her better, asking some of the questions that had been burning holes in his mind.

Apparently, he had asked too much. With an inward sigh, he decided to take her obvious hint and focus on business, at least for the moment.

"I'm not sure they're actually discrepancies." He bent over to reach in the folds of the briefcase that rested on the floor next to his chair. He pulled out the Sheffield file and opened it to the relevant document. "I noticed that Harrison made several large payments to service consultants, but, unlike most of the accounts, there isn't a very thorough record of the payments."

Sliding the open file across the table to her, he pointed to the information on the page. "See? Wentworth & Schultz. The payments were recorded in the books, but I can't find any record of contracts for the services or anything on what the payments were actually for." He braced himself for a reaction—afraid she would call his bluff and expose his reason for lunch as the weak excuse it was.

Instead, her unreadable, businesslike expression stayed fixed. "I'm unfamiliar with those particular consultants."

Ah, she was giving him the careful answer. She was good. Better suited to law than what she was doing.

"I'm sure it will be a simple matter to get the receipts or copies of the contracts for you."

He barely listened to her cool tone. He was wondering what it would take to see that spark of humor, which had glinted when he teased her about Scrabble, return to her eyes. He didn't know, but he was determined to find out.

The waiter arrived with their food, and Nye quickly slid the folder back to him. Cullen observed her defensive demeanor while the waiter put their plates on the table. She may think she had shut him out, but he wasn't going to be scared off so easily. Every glimpse he got of the person hiding behind the rigid walls, beneath the shadow of pain, made him all the more desperate to break through her defenses. It might not be today, or even tomorrow, but he wouldn't give up until he found a way into her heart.

Chapter Ten

*"Anyone who says sunshine brings happiness
has never danced in the rain."*
– Author Unknown

Still rattled from her lunch with Cullen an hour earlier, Nye was in no condition for a crisis of conscience. Nevertheless, that's what she was facing as she sat at her desk, staring at the contract for the purchase of Russell Flanagan's property. She should have called Russell by now or stopped at his home. Normally, she would never let so much time pass during an attempted sale. This was a rare case. She was stuck.

She had seen the resolve in Russell's eyes when he insisted on the stipulation against casino building. There would be no point in trying to convince him to sell unless she agreed to that. But what could she do without approval from her superiors? She wasn't even going to consider that Dan had been suggesting anything other than ethical methods of persuasion when he insisted Nye get the sale.

She pressed her face into her hands and grunted in frustration.

A soft rap sounded at the door. Nye looked up at Brianna.

"Mr. Akkerman's out of the meeting. He'll see you now."

Nye shoved her chair back with a sigh and stood. "Thanks."

She walked into the hallway, briefly entertaining the idea of asking Dan to change his mind about Russell. She immediately dismissed the thought as the wishful thinking it was. All of the principals at this firm, probably in private equity as a whole, were much too focused on profit to respect an elderly man's faith-based principles.

"Go on in." Rachel, seated behind her desk, motioned to Dan's office door.

"Thanks." Nye knocked as she entered.

Dan looked up from his work, and smiled when he spotted her. "Nye. Just the person I wanted to see." He waved her over to the desk. "Have a seat."

She approached but didn't sit. "I won't take up your time. I just need to ask you about some—"

"Nye, please," he interrupted, still smiling. "I'm your boss, and I'm telling you to have a seat. Whatever work you have to do can wait."

She reluctantly sat in the chair opposite his desk.

"I wanted to congratulate you on the progress you're making with Sheffield. I hear you've all but wrapped up the sale—and in record time, too."

She leaned forward. "That's what I wanted to talk to you about."

"Oh?"

"Yes, the lawyer for the purchasing company has asked for more documentation on some payments recorded in the Harrison books. The company apparently made several payments to Wentworth & Schultz service consultants, but there are no receipts to show what the services were."

Dan fiddled with a folder on his desk. "Mm-hmm."

Annoyed by his apparent boredom, she tried to meet his eyes. As she often had to do, she reminded herself that being the son of a named principal in the firm didn't automatically mean Dan had inherited a temperament suited for the business. "I had never heard of Wentworth & Schultz. Are you familiar with the organization?"

He cleared his throat. "Yes, I've dealt with them. But why are you bringing this to me? It seems like something you can handle. Did you ask the treasurer?"

Nye's irritation grew at the implication that she wasn't handling her job properly. "Yes, and she said the payments were for services performed for our firm in connection with Harrison. She said you handled the contract and didn't give her a receipt when she asked for it."

"Oh, yeah." He looked at Nye, then glanced away. "I remember that. It was somehow lost in the cycles of paperwork around here. I was going to get her another copy." He met Nye's gaze and smiled. "Don't worry. I'll contact the … Wentworth, did you say? I'll talk to them and get the receipts."

"Thank you," she replied automatically, but a strange feeling started to creep up on her. She tried to shrug it off, reminding herself the situation was just a result of Dan's cavalier approach to business. She stood and turned to go.

"Wait a minute, Nye."

She faced him.

"I wanted to tell you that I'm leaving for vacation next week. I'll be gone for quite a while."

"Oh?" She raised her eyebrows, surprised this was the first she had heard of it. Principals at their firm usually planned extended vacations at least a year in advance. "Where are you going?"

He stood and meandered around the desk, putting his hands in his pockets. "The Bahamas." He smiled impishly. "I'd ask you to go with me, but …"

She raised an eyebrow. He sobered. "I'd like you to wrap up the Harrison sale before I leave. I don't want to leave any loose ends behind."

She didn't like this uncomfortable sensation creeping up her spine. She nodded. "I'll do what I can."

He flashed a broad smile. "Great. I knew I could count on you."

She exited the office, the odd premonition clinging to her like a spider web. There was nothing really wrong with anything he had said. Papers did get lost, and people did go on vacations. But as she walked down the hall, she couldn't shake the feeling that her world was once again starting to tremble.

Nye jerked when the shrill ring of the phone cut through the silence. She peered at the clock on the wall, surprised at how dark her office had become. It was almost five after nine. She glanced at the caller ID display on her desk phone as it rang again.

An unfamiliar number. Strange. No one but a family member would ordinarily call her at work after business hours.

She lifted the receiver. "Hello?"

"Nye?" Cullen's deep voice carried over the line.

She nearly dropped the receiver. "Yes?" She choked out the word, trying to recover from her surprise. She had been prepared to be distant and reserved with him the next time they met, but she hadn't expected a phone call.

"Somehow I knew you'd still be at the office." He chuckled.

She forced herself to breathe evenly, trying to calm the ridiculous tingling sensation that shot through her at the sound of his deep laugh. "Guilty as charged," she replied, pleased with how controlled she sounded.

"Well, you're not the only one."

"You're still at work?" She turned away from the desk as her gaze involuntarily went to the window, searching for the tall building that housed his office.

"Afraid so."

Soft light glowed from a few outside offices on the higher floors of the State Bank building.

"I'm sorry to call so late," he continued, "but I need to talk to you about something."

She sucked in a breath, bracing herself.

"It's about the Sheffield deal."

She breathed again. "Oh." She tried to ignore the disappointment that mixed with her relief as she gazed at a corner window in the skyscraper, wondering if that was his office. Her emotions were such a jumbled mass of confusion these days.

It was just business, she reminded herself. Focus.

"Can you come to my office?"

Her concentration deflated with a whoosh as she swung back to the desk and leaned forward. "Now?" She tried not to sound as flabbergasted as she felt.

"Yes. It's important."

She pictured being alone with Cullen in his office. Pushing down rising panic at the image, she summoned the strength that had gotten her through much worse. "I'm sorry, but I have a lot of work to get through yet tonight." She kept her voice even and firm. "Perhaps we can discuss it in the morning."

"It can't wait 'til then."

Her resolve dwindled as the haunting premonition that she had felt in Dan's office returned. "Is something wrong?" she asked, almost afraid to hear the answer.

"Yes. Something is very wrong."

"I'll be right there."

The elevator doors opened on the top floor of the State Bank building. Nye's heart did its traditional flip at the sight of Cullen, waiting for her, hands in his pockets. Accustomed to his appearance during business hours, Nye was surprised to see him without a suit jacket, his shirt sleeves rolled up to reveal muscled forearms. Despite her determination to keep this meeting professional, she couldn't help but notice the attractive way the open neck of his white shirt contrasted with his dark features.

"Thanks for coming." His slight smile was tense, as she stepped off the elevator.

"Sure." Her apprehension returned.

"My office is this way."

She followed him as they passed a large desk, where, she assumed, a receptionist must sit during business hours. They turned a corner and continued down a hallway, dimly lit and eerily quiet—an atmosphere that only amplified Nye's growing anxiety. Light filtered under the closed door of one office, but the others were dark and empty.

They reached an open door, and she braced herself—for what, she didn't know.

Cullen stood to the side to let her enter first. The office held dark, tasteful furniture, including a huge desk, buried under stacks of papers. More piles of folders and documents sat precariously in the extra chairs that faced the desk.

"Sorry about the mess. Things have been pretty crazy lately. You're driving a hard pace with the Sheffield deal." He smiled, but his eyes were missing their usual twinkle.

Nye was tired of the guessing game. "You said there was something wrong. What is it?"

He turned away and moved a stack of papers off one of the chairs. "Please, sit down." He walked around his desk.

The tension in his demeanor fueled her misgivings. Instead of sitting, she walked to his desk. "Cullen, what is it?"

He met her gaze as if startled to hear her say his name.

She realized with a surge of her pulse that it was the first time she had ever spoken his first name. She hadn't consciously intended the familiar gesture, and she wished he hadn't noticed.

She was relieved when the flash of warmth in his gaze faded, as he glanced down at an open file folder on his desk.

"It's about those payments to Wentworth & Schultz."

"What about them?" Her breathing quickened. "Didn't Brianna give you my message? I spoke with the principal involved, and he said he'd get the receipts for you. I just don't have them yet."

He nodded. "Yes, I know. I got the message, but …" He sank into his desk chair.

Her mind whirled with possibilities. What didn't he want to tell her?

"I did some more digging on my own. The bank account that the Harrison Company's payments went to is under the name of Wentworth & Schultz. I found out that these service consultants are supposedly based in the Bahamas."

Nye's mouth went dry. Still, it could mean nothing. "You doubt it?" She laced her tone with cynicism and suspicion. She couldn't help it. Survival instincts put her on the defensive, telling her to play the game that characterized the masters of this business world.

He locked her gaze with his own. "I contacted the government there and asked about Wentworth & Schultz." He paused. "Nye, the company is set up under the name of Dan Akkerman."

Her legs weakened, and she sank into the empty chair. "What?"

His eyes held concern as he watched her. "I'm sorry. I've double checked and triple checked. I don't want to falsely accuse anyone."

"But what are you saying … fraud? Dan?" She tried to grasp the idea. No. He had to be wrong. She shook her head. "I'm sure there must be some other explanation."

He leaned forward. "I hope there is. But it doesn't look good."

She stared at the floor, struggling to make sense of what he said. Securities fraud? Right under her nose? Impossible.

She looked up. "Do you have any proof? Any documentation?"

"Of course." He pushed a folder toward her.

Nye lifted the file from his desk.

"The authorities in the Bahamas faxed me information on the company."

She intently examined the documents. With each revelation, her breathing quickened.

"You'll notice it lists Dan Akkerman as the company's founder."

A sinking feeling started in her throat and dropped to her stomach as she saw the name and company information. If Cullen's suspicions were correct, it would mean disaster. KBA would be investigated, shut down. She would lose her job and her credibility—everything she had worked so hard to build.

She was the firm's manager; she couldn't possibly have missed something like this. There had to be an alternate explanation. It didn't have to mean Dan had siphoned the money for himself.

"I'll have to inform the authorities."

She jumped inwardly at the sound of Cullen's voice at her side. He had rounded the desk while she was thinking.

He looked down at her, concern again in his eyes. "I wanted to tell you first."

She looked away. "Thank you." She paused. "Can you … wait?"

His brow furrowed with confusion.

"I think there could be some other explanation. I'd like to look into things myself. Perhaps talk to Dan."

"Are you sure that's wise? You don't know how he might react."

"I just can't believe he'd do something like that." What she really couldn't believe was that she could have been so taken in and not have detected his criminal activity. There had to be a way to salvage things, to save KBA and herself. "Just a little more time." She stood, ending up much closer to Cullen than she anticipated. With only inches between them, she was caught in a magnetic force of awareness.

His breathing deepened, matching hers.

"Please?" she whispered, staring at his shirt front.

He slowly lifted his hand to touch her face.

She jolted back. She glanced at the window, the wall, anywhere but at him.

"I'm sorry … I—"

"Thank you for the information." She tried to sound professional, while every muscle in her body screamed at her to sprint for the door. "But I'm sure there's nothing wrong with the finances. Dan will have some explanation." She reached the door and fumbled for the knob.

"Nye, wait—"

"Good night." She rushed into the hallway and hurried to the elevator in a haze. She had caught a look in his eyes as she bolted—another emotion she hadn't seen there before. Pain. Her life was about to crumble and what bothered her most was that she had hurt Cullen.

Nye swept out of the conference room the moment the morning meeting at Sheffield let out. She rushed for the stairs, hoping Cullen was still caught answering Van Vechten's questions.

She swung the door open to the stairs and someone grabbed it.

Cullen held the door with one hand, his mouth in a grim line that matched the ones on his brow. "We need to talk."

Not sure what to say, she walked through the doorway and waited for him on the staircase landing.

He stopped in front of her, letting the door shut behind them. "That was very uncomfortable in there. Maybe wrong. I'm sorry, but I can't keep quiet about this any longer."

She swallowed the guilt that clogged her throat. "I know. I had to come to the meeting first thing this morning, so I haven't been able to talk to Dan yet. I'm going to do that now."

"You're still convinced he has an explanation?"

She couldn't meet his gaze. "I hope so."

"Okay. Let's go then." He started down the stairs.

"What?" Shock kept her where she was.

He stopped and looked back. "I'm going with you."

"You don't trust me?"

"I don't trust him. If he's guilty of what I think he is, there's no telling what he'll do if you confront him with it. Don't you ever watch murder mysteries?"

Ignoring his stab at humor, she started down the stairs next to him. "That's very nice, but I have to do this alone. He's far more likely to take offense or not tell me the truth if you're with me."

"Guess that's a risk we'll have to take."

Biting her tongue, Nye marched down the steps. She couldn't stop him from following her to KBA, but she wouldn't be treated like a helpless victim. It was as if Cullen was determined to think the worst and ruin her livelihood by his ill-formed conclusions. He just might be disappointed. If Nye's life was going to be overturned again, this time it wouldn't happen without a fight.

Nye wiped her sweating palm against her skirt as she waited.

Rachel looked up from her desk with a perplexed smile.

"He might be a while yet. Are you sure you want to wait here?"

"I'm sure. Thanks." Nye went to the other side of the waiting area outside Dan's office. Cullen stood with his back to the large window, watching her. She stared past him, seeing nothing through the glass but her jumbled thoughts and worries. She clutched the file Cullen had given her, filled with the incriminating evidence.

"I still think I should go with you." Cullen's voice was low and quiet.

It had a surprisingly calming effect on her nerves. "You'll be able to hear if anything goes wrong."

When they arrived at KBA, Nye had actually considered calling security to get rid of Cullen. Deciding that was a little too drastic, she had managed to convince him to stay in the waiting area just outside Dan's office.

"Nye," Rachel said from the desk, "he can see you now."

"Thank you." Nye headed for the office door.

"If you're in there too long, I'm coming in." Cullen's expression said there'd be no talking him out of that promise.

Nye nodded. His concern was sweet, yet she couldn't help but think she wouldn't even be in this situation if not for him.

She knocked softly on Dan's door and entered the office.

Dan was leaning back in his chair with his feet on the desk, looking as carefree and casual as always. "My favorite employee." He grinned. "Set yourself down and tell me the big news." He dropped his legs and shifted forward. "You made the sale, didn't you?"

She stared at him.

"Come on, don't keep me hanging. You made the Sheffield deal, right?"

She cleared her throat and slowly sat in the chair he had indicated. "No, that's not what I wanted to see you about. Not exactly."

"Ah, the lady of mystery." His levity didn't lessen as he tipped back again, lacing his fingers behind his head. "You want me to guess?"

"No."

"Aw, you're no fun."

"Mr. Akkerman," Nye began.

"Still 'mister'?"

Tired of the games and her own hesitation, she took a breath and met his joking gaze with her grim one. "There have been some discoveries regarding the Harrison Company, and they don't look good."

"Don't look good?" His smile faltered.

"Suspicious might be more accurate." She held up the file. "This folder contains documents for the payments to Wentworth & Schultz that you said you would deal with."

"Right. And I'm going to. It's not exactly top priority for someone in my position, Nye," he said, in a condescending tone she had never heard him use before.

She didn't like the doubts that flared in her mind as his

demeanor started to change. But the shift acted like fuel that burned through her reluctance to accuse him. She set the folder on his desk and flicked it open. "Wentworth & Schultz is in the Bahamas. And you're listed as the founder." She spun the file around to face him and pointed her finger at his name printed on the page.

He stared at the document.

Nye's hopes sank as she watched the color drain from his face. She moistened her lips. "Tell me there's some reasonable explanation for this."

His gaze flitted to her face then away. He turned in the chair, leaving her to stare at its tall leather back. "Is it unreasonable to want something more than living in daddy's shadow forever?" He swiveled to face her, his face twisted with emotion. "I just want to be free. Can't you understand that?"

She couldn't speak.

"I didn't hurt anyone. You know that. Can't you just let it go?" He stood and came around the desk. He crouched in front of her.

"Think of all the people you'd be hurting if you tell anyone. Not just me. Everyone would lose their jobs. You, too. Think about it."

His pleading voice was like an echo of the one inside her. Why was this happening? Why did it all have to be destroyed over something so minor? He was right. He had only taken a comparatively small amount from people so wealthy they would never miss it or even know they had lost anything. Would it really do any harm to just let it go? So many lives would be turned upside down if the truth were exposed.

"Please, Nye?" Dan suddenly grabbed Nye's hands from her lap and clutched them, still crouched at her knees. "No one has to know."

"But I know."

Nye jerked her head around to see Cullen enter the office. She quickly pulled her hands from Dan's grasp and stood, as did Dan. How long had Cullen been there?

"Who are you?" Dan's eyes narrowed as he sized up Cullen.

"Sheffield's lawyer."

"He knows?" Dan looked at Nye as if she had betrayed him.

"He's the one who found the ..."

"Evidence," Cullen finished. "I take it there wasn't an alternative explanation." He stared at Nye, keen disappointment reflected in the gaze that felt like an arrow shot dead-center into her heart.

She looked away.

"I'll report what I've found immediately." Cullen looked at Dan, who sagged on the edge of his desk, slumped and defeated.

Nye couldn't stand it. Why did Dan have to be so stupid? And why did Cullen have to be so righteous? She left the room, wanting to break into a run when she reached the hall.

A hand grabbed her arm. "Nye, wait." Cullen kept a hold on her as if afraid she'd flee.

She couldn't look at his face.

"What happened back there … Just how close are you to him?"

She met his gaze and saw an aching vulnerability—that glint of pain. Perhaps it would be better to let him think there was something between her and Dan. Maybe then he wouldn't care so much, and she could be safe again.

He slowly let go of her arm.

She stared at the floor, not wanting to see what his eyes held now.

"I'm sorry," he said, as he backed away.

So was she.

Chapter Eleven

*"All that is made seems planless to the darkened mind, because
there are more plans than it looked for ...
So with the Great Dance."*
–C. S. Lewis

Nye set the pencil holder in the cardboard box on her desk. She scanned the clean desktop, bare walls, empty bookcase—making sure she wasn't missing anything. Not that she had anything to miss. She probably wouldn't have even needed a box to carry her meager belongings out of the office.

She went to the window for a last look at the view.

Exposed fraud in movies or on television was always so dramatic, shrouded with intrigue. In real life, the experience was better described as lackluster. Nye hadn't seen Dan dragged away in handcuffs or anything so unpleasant. He had just quietly disappeared—there one moment, gone the next. KBA was a thriving, sixty-year-old firm on Monday and closed for investigation of securities fraud before the weekend.

Immediately after Cullen had reported his findings, the Federal authorities shut down KBA and questioned all of the firm's employees. Nye had only been subjected to one brief investigative interview. Once they realized how little she had known about Dan's actions, the investigators excused her from further questioning.

They found no evidence to implicate anyone other than Dan in the fraud, and only he was in custody, waiting to stand trial. KBA would likely be allowed to resume operations soon, but the firm's reputation had been irreparably damaged. Trying to extract herself from the disagreeable situation as swiftly as possible, Nye had resigned—a move most of the employees were duplicating.

Nye turned away from the window with a sigh and picked up the box. Resting it on her hip, she walked to the door and flicked the light switch, not looking back.

Voices carried into the hallway from Renee's office. Nye paused, tempted to duck out without being seen. Resisting the urge, she turned and headed for the open office door. She wished these farewells weren't so obligatory, but she didn't want to be thought of as rude or heartless, even if only by people she never expected to see again after today.

She peered into the office where Brianna helped Renee pack her belongings. Nye raised her eyebrows, surprised at the number of full boxes on the floor and desk. She stepped into the room. "How's it going?"

Renee and Brianna looked up.

Nye tried not to cringe at their watery eyes and the red puffiness of their faces. She had been afraid they would get emotional.

"Okay." Renee sniffled and wiped her nose with a crumpled tissue. "Are you done already?"

"I didn't have much."

"You're leaving?" Brianna looked at her with a drippy sadness that held no trace of the professionalism that used to dominate her features. "Right now?"

"Afraid so." Nye smiled gently. "I thought I'd stop and say good-bye."

"Oh …" The word came out with a sob, as Brianna went to Nye and gave her a hug.

Nye awkwardly returned the embrace.

"You were a great boss." Brianna stepped back and wiped at a fresh tear that trickled down her cheek.

Nye mustered a sympathetic smile. "Thank you. You're the best assistant I've ever had."

Brianna brightened at the compliment. "Thanks."

"Me, too!" Renee approached Nye with her arms outstretched.

Nye gripped the box under her arm as she hugged the sniffling woman.

"You were wonderful to work with, Nye. Just wonderful." Renee smiled through the pools in her eyes as she pulled away.

"You, too." Nye felt some remorse that she couldn't infuse her voice with greater sincerity or sentiment. She didn't mean to be cold, but she couldn't conjure up more emotion than she actually felt.

"I'll miss you, Nye. Take care." Renee gave Nye a last squeeze.

"See you again sometime?" Brianna asked.

"Maybe. Good luck." Nye gave a little wave as she turned and exited the room, feeling nothing but relief that the partings were over. She had no sense of loss when she left her office for the last time and didn't feel a trace of sadness during the good-byes, made tearful only by her coworkers. She had thought losing her job would be the start of her life crumbling again, but it wasn't. Now that she was at this point, she really felt fine with the turn of events.

As she headed for the front door, satisfaction welled within her, adding buoyancy to her step. She had succeeded in foiling an attack meant to rattle her world. God apparently wasn't through with whatever game He was playing with her life. Perhaps she was doing too well living without tango, without Dante. God wanted to shake her up again, take her out at the knees and see how much a person could endure.

She was ready for Him this time. She wouldn't be broken again. Her survival plan had worked beautifully. Since she had purposefully avoided developing any passion for her work or emotional attachments to coworkers and clients, she was safe from any real harm when her job collapsed. She did not feel any pangs of loss, any resentment, or sense of betrayal from Dan's actions.

The one element of this affair that inspired anything close to regret was the loss of a reason to visit Russell Flanagan. At least she no longer had to deal with the conflict between KBA and Russell's scruples. Given the fondness she seemed to have developed for the old gentleman, Nye had decided to see him one more time and tell him about KBA in person.

Despite that one, small ripple in her strict emotional detachment, Nye was proud of herself. She could easily leave Russell once she had said good-bye and, with no serious emotions involved, she would lose nothing vital with the collapse of the firm. Even if her reputation as a private equity manager was damaged, with her skills and experience, she could easily find employment in any other area of business.

Even her misunderstanding with Cullen had a positive side. Now that he thought she was involved with a thief and ready to hide Dan's crimes, Cullen had been keeping his distance. Nye hadn't seen him since that day in Dan's office, and she was relieved that she didn't have to worry about dealing with him anymore. He had already caused more problems than she had anticipated or wanted.

Yet relief wasn't what she felt when she remembered his face, dark eyes full of hurt and disappointment. Or the times before, when they had lit up with happiness and maybe something more as he looked at her.

She pushed through the door into the frigid outdoors. Bitterness surged in her throat, swallowing up the unwanted twinge of grief. God could go ahead and take her job. And He could take Cullen. He had caused her greater pain three years ago than she would have thought possible. No one, not Cullen, and not even God, would ever be able to hurt her that much again.

Nye sipped the coffee Russell served to her.

"Why don't you work for me?"

Nye lowered her mug, staring at Russell. A job invitation was not the response she had expected when she told him about the collapse of KBA. She was more than a little confused by the delight in his eyes as he watched her from his armchair. She swallowed and found her voice. "What do you mean?"

"You could look over these offers I'm getting. Go through them for me and make sure they're all right."

She leaned against the back of the soft sofa and shook her head, a small smile curving her lips. "It's very sweet of you to offer, but I don't think that will be necessary. I should be able to find another job easily enough."

He frowned. "It isn't a handout. I don't often say this, but I could use some help. I need someone to make sure I don't get tricked into selling to some sharks. I don't always understand all that gibberish they put in those contracts."

Nye took a moment to consider what he was asking. She did like this sweet man. For some reason, she was more at peace in his company than anywhere else, and from the moment she had met him, she felt as if they shared an indefinable bond. The truth was that she had become attached, something she never allowed to happen. No, as much as she would welcome a reason to continue her friendship with Russell, she couldn't risk the inevitable result. He was old, and the painful loss of such a friend was even more assured than with other relationships.

"I'm so flattered you'd consider me," she answered, "but I only have a business degree. What you really need for this kind of work is a good lawyer."

"I don't need a lawyer."

"If it's a matter of money, I can give you some recommendations for relatively inexpensive legal help."

He met her gaze and spoke more emphatically. "I don't need a lawyer. You gave me one of those contracts yourself—you know enough to check them over, make sure I don't get cheated."

He was right. She did have enough expertise for the assistance he needed, but she had to make a clean break while she still could. "I'm sorry, Mr. Flanagan, but I must refuse." She kept her voice firm. "You really do need to hire a lawyer if you require any help."

Disappointment flashed in his eyes, and he looked away. He absently rubbed his shortened leg.

Concern softened Nye's resistance. "Does it hurt?"

"At my age, everything hurts." He smiled slightly, as if trying to ease her worry.

She didn't want it to end like this. She couldn't walk away from him feeling like a heel who had rejected such a kind soul. How could she cheer him or at least turn his mind to other things? Her gaze fell on the chess set still assembled on the coffee table.

She leaned forward and smiled at the intricate figures. "Do you like chess?"

"Used to. Don't really play much now."

"But you leave it out?" She raised her eyebrows in question.

"It's waiting."

She glanced at the chess board. "Waiting?"

"For my grandson. We used to play every day. When he gets time, he'll stop by, and we'll do it again."

The story sounded so familiar. She raised a startled gaze to Russell's dark brown eyes, so like ... It couldn't be possible, could it? She licked her lips, her mouth dry. "What is your grandson's name?"

Russell tilted his head. "Cullen. Cullen Chandler."

Nye sagged back against the sofa. "Unbelievable." It explained so much—the familiarity of his eyes, his mannerisms, gestures. Russell Flanagan was the grandfather who had done so much for Cullen and his brother? It fit so well, she could have kicked herself for not realizing the connection sooner.

"Are you doing all right?" Russell watched her.

"I know your grandson. We worked together on the deal that just fell through. He was the attorney who discovered the fraud."

His eyes wide, Russell looked as astonished as Nye felt. "Well, I'll be. The Lord works in mysterious ways. You two are friends then?"

She hesitated, hating herself for the blush that warmed her cheeks. "Yes, I guess you could say we became friends."

"Maybe even a little more than that?"

She quickly looked away from the twinkling eyes that hid his shrewdness. "We were on opposing sides of a business deal, Mr. Flanagan." She forced herself to steadily meet his gaze. "Anything more than friendship would have been inappropriate."

"I think you should start calling me Russell. If you're friends with my grandson that makes you one of the family." His pleased grin told her he didn't believe her answer.

She should have known better than to try to hide anything since he somehow always managed to read her true feelings. Well, two could play that game, and she smelled something suspicious.

She fixed him with a firm gaze. "Okay, Russell. If Cullen is your grandson, why did you tell me you don't have a lawyer?" She couldn't help feeling some satisfaction as he looked slightly uncomfortable.

"I don't like to bother him."

"Bother him? You mean you didn't ask him for help?" Realization dawned. "Cullen does know that you're selling, right?"

He pressed his lips together and shook his head.

"Russell! Why didn't you tell him? I'm sure he would help. In fact, I'm sure he would insist on representing you and looking at the contracts—all of that. Why in the world wouldn't you tell him something like this?" She stared at Russell.

He grabbed his coffee mug as if needing something to do. He ran his thumb along its edge and looked into the liquid it held. "He's so busy … working on important things."

Nye didn't like the insinuation that Russell's sale was less important than any corporation's deal.

Before she could comment, he continued. "Cullen has worked hard his whole life, taking on so much, trying to help everybody and fix everything." He stared ahead into an unseen memory. "He was a wonder, even as a boy. I've always been proud of him." He took in a long breath and let it out. "I know he'd help me if I asked, but I don't want to bother anyone."

"That's not fair."

He turned a startled gaze to her.

"Cullen would want to know about this." She leaned forward. "I'm sure he cares much more about you than his other work. You need to tell him."

Russell tilted his chin, his jaw stubbornly set. He shook his head.

"Then let me."

He stared at her, unrelenting.

"Please?" She spoke the word softly.

At length, a smile slowly broke through the resolve. "Honey, you could melt ice in the dead of winter. I can see why my grandson likes you."

She tried to ignore the heat that involuntarily sprang to her face again. "Does that mean it's all right if I tell him?"

He hesitated, then nodded.

She let out the breath she hadn't realized she was holding. "Good." Apprehension came on the heels of her relief, as she became aware of what she had just said she would do.

Just when she had gotten Cullen a safe distance away, even voluntarily staying far from her, she had to go and create a reason to reopen the lines of communication. What was she thinking? Oriana would have a field day with the subconscious implications of such a mistake, if Nye were stupid enough to tell her.

Realizing how long she had been silent, Nye looked up to see Russell sitting motionless, staring at the coffee table.

Resolving to put her personal troubles aside, she smiled, determined to brighten his spirits if she could. "How about one game before I go?" She gestured to the chess board.

The eagerness in his eyes as he quickly took her up on the offer brought her both pleasure and a wave of concern. It might not be as easy as she had thought to walk out of Russell's life and never see him again. She didn't know what it was about their family, but Cullen and Russell were two of a kind—men who, in different but irresistible ways, were slowly stealing her heart.

Cullen reached for the ringing cell phone. Not even a twinge of guilt for taking a personal call this time—it was after business hours, and he was desperate for a break. Sure it was his mother, he didn't check before answering.

"Hello?"

"Cullen?"

His breath caught.

"This is Nye Sanders."

As if he wouldn't recognize the voice he had been longing to hear. "Hi. Good to hear from you." He hoped the understatement sounded more nonchalant than he felt. His heart raced at Kentucky Derby pace as a chaos of emotions battled in his mind. He had wanted to call her after everything that had happened, but he had no clue what to say or how to act. He wasn't even sure how he felt anymore.

"How are you?" he asked. The question sounded so inappropriate. How did he think she was? She just lost her job and her boyfriend, thanks to him. He felt so stupid for never having thought of the possibility that she had a boyfriend already. Her mother hadn't mentioned it, but maybe she didn't know.

"I'm doing well, thanks. And you?"

Her reply was automatic, not a true reflection of what she was going through. He shouldn't expect anything different. From what he overheard of her conversation with Dan that day, he feared Nye was actually thinking of not reporting the fraud. He didn't want to even consider that. If it were true, she would blame him all the more for KBA's collapse. He didn't feel bad about reporting what he found, but he had done battle with guilty feelings every day since for being the cause of pain to Nye. Maybe this call was his chance to try to make amends for that, at least.

He cleared his throat. "I've been meaning to call you."

There was a pause. "You have?"

He leaned back in his chair. "I wanted to apologize. I feel really bad about what happened ... with KBA, I mean. And Dan. I'm sorry I had to be the one to find out."

More silence. "You did what you had to do."

His heart sank. She did blame him.

"I know you're probably working, so I'll get to the point

of my call."

"Yes?" He braced himself, not sure what to expect. A lawsuit? He shook his head at his lawyer's cynicism. He may have misjudged Nye somewhat, but he couldn't believe he had been that blind as to her character.

"It's about your grandfather."

"Granddad?" It was the last thing he had expected her to say. "You know him?"

"Yes. I didn't know you were related 'til today. I met him several weeks ago when I tried to buy his land for KBA."

"Buy his land? That's impossible. Granddad would never sell the ranch."

"He's going to have to." Her voice softened as she continued. "His land is being annexed into the city, and he can't afford the changes they're requiring."

Cullen tried to process the news. "I can't believe it … I had no idea."

"I know." The understanding in her voice was like a comforting balm to his shock. "I told him he was wrong to keep all this from you. I knew you'd try to help him if you were aware of what was going on."

"Of course," he murmured, as irritation started to overcome his surprise. Why hadn't his grandfather told him about any of this? In all fairness, he supposed he hadn't really given his grandfather much of a chance to keep him informed. Cullen had been too busy and not accessible enough, but he had called a number of times. It almost seemed like his grandfather had intentionally kept the sale hidden from Cullen. Why would he do such a thing?

"I hope I didn't overstep my place by telling you, but I thought you should know."

"No, I appreciate it. I should probably call him right away." He hated to end the long-awaited conversation with Nye so abruptly, but his mind was swimming with new troubles.

"Oh, of course. I'll let you go."

"And Nye?"

"Yes?"

"Thank you."

He savored the sound of her voice as she said good-bye. If only the reason she called hadn't been so difficult to swallow. He sighed and selected his grandfather's number from the menu on his cell phone.

Five minutes later, he was even more frustrated. "Granddad, it wouldn't be a bother at all. You should know that. Did you tell Mom and Dad?"

"It never came up."

"Granddad!" Cullen tried to rein in his exasperation. He had never felt anything even close to anger at his grandfather before. He spotted the photo of his grandfather and his horse, an image that made him remember the man who had patiently taught two young boys how to ride and how to live. He took a breath and tried a new approach. "Will you let us help? Can we pay for the changes the city wants?"

"Of course not. I won't hear of it."

Calming enough to think more rationally, Cullen realized what his grandfather meant. "It's too much, isn't it? Too expensive to pay."

"I'm afraid so."

Cullen sighed. His grandfather owned a huge chunk of land—of course it would cost a small fortune to prepare so much property for inclusion in the city. "Where will you go?"

"I'll find a nice little house somewhere. In the country—if there's any place left that's not city anymore." He coughed. "You can tell your mom, bless her heart, that I'm not moving in with her and your dad."

A smile crept onto Cullen's face at his grandfather's stubborn tone. "That's why you haven't told her about the sale, isn't it?"

"Well, you know she'd insist on it."

Cullen couldn't deny the truth of that statement. His mother worried incessantly about her dad living alone, so far away from her. Cullen's proximity to his grandfather was supposed to ease her concern, but he had evidently been failing that responsibility.

"All right, Granddad, you win, but I'm going to help with the legal aspect, okay? I want to look at any offers you get from now on."

"Fair enough."

"Good. And will you promise to tell me the next time anything serious happens? I'd rather not find out about it from someone else."

"I didn't think you'd mind getting a call from Nye."

Cullen could hear the smile in his grandfather's voice. "You wouldn't be matchmaking, would you, Granddad?"

"Sounds to me like the Lord already did the matchmaking. She told me you know each other."

"Yes, we do." Cullen barely resisted the urge to ask what else she had said. "But it's just a professional relationship." Better to quash any ideas right away, his grandfather's and his own.

"Really? She said you were friends."

Cullen's heart did an involuntary leap. Especially after everything that had happened, he wouldn't have hoped to qualify as a friend in her mind.

"I'm guessing it might be more than that. Am I right?"

Cullen sighed. His grandfather always had an uncanny knack for reading people's thoughts or maybe just their desires. "I don't know, Granddad. It's … complicated."

"Never too complicated for the Lord." He paused. "Just don't stop loving her."

Loving her? Cullen knew he felt something very strong for Nye, something that grew every day, but love? Perhaps a friendship kind of love was all that his grandfather meant.

Whatever Cullen felt for Nye, he was fairly certain that, even if he wanted to, he would never be able to stop.

Chapter Twelve

"I would believe only in a God that knows how to dance."
– Friedrich Nietzsche

Nye froze at the sound of the front door opening.

"Hello? Anybody home?" Her mother's voice carried into the dining room where Nye sat at the table.

She swallowed the last bite of toast with a frown as Jordan trotted out of the room to meet her mother. So much for a leisurely breakfast. Taking a deep breath, she mustered a more pleasant response than she felt. "In the dining room," she called.

"There's my beautiful boy. How are you?"

Nye listened to her mother greet Jordan in the other room, glad she had time to prepare herself. It had been more than two weeks since she quit her job, and her mother still wouldn't let up. As soon as her parents had learned what happened, Mother's maternal instincts seemed to quadruple in strength, and she was suffocating Nye with her efforts to simultaneously comfort and control.

Before Nye felt truly ready, her mother's smiling face appeared in the doorway to the kitchen. The cheerful expression wavered when she spotted Nye sitting at the table, drinking coffee. Jordan pushed past her, his tail wagging.

Mother titled her head—her unconscious habit when anything puzzled or surprised her. "You're just eating breakfast now? It's eleven thirty."

Nye took a sip of coffee, hoping her irritation would wash down with the liquid. She lowered the mug. "I slept late." In truth, she hadn't really slept at all until early in the morning. The nightmares had returned with the dreadful regularity of those first months after Dante's death.

Mother shook her head as she walked to the counter and set down the grocery bag she carried. "Well, I brought you some meals." She reached into the bag and began pulling out foil-wrapped platters of homemade dishes. "There's lasagna. I know that's your favorite. There's also egg salad, tuna salad—"

"What are you doing?" Nye rose and went to the counter.

Her mother stopped and looked up, her head tilted again.

"I'm not sick, I'm unemployed. I can still make my own food."

Her mother squared her shoulders and grabbed the refrigerator door. "I know that." She started swiftly transferring the containers to the refrigerator. "But I'm sure you're busy looking for a new job. That's time-consuming, stressful. This will be one less thing you'll need to worry about." She smiled and held up a cake pan. "I even brought chocolate cheesecake."

Nye sighed, giving up. Oriana would never forgive her if she turned away their mother's homemade food.

"How's the job search going?" She put the cheesecake in the refrigerator.

"It's only been a couple weeks." Nye mentally chided herself for her defensive attitude. It became an instinctive reaction when her mother behaved this way. Reminding herself that Mother only meddled because she cared, Nye tried to be more patient. "I've applied to a few places, but they don't look very good. There's really not that much available right now. At least not in Harper."

Her mother jerked out of the refrigerator to look at Nye. "You wouldn't move?"

Nye paused and watched Jordan lie on the kitchen floor, buying time before she answered. She was treading on sensitive ground. "I don't know. I'll have to see where the job opportunities are."

"You aren't going to run away again, are you?"

The question hung in the air as Nye fought to control the anger that rose in response to the accusation. She swallowed the bitter taste in her mouth. "I didn't run, Mother."

"You left New York. You gave up tango—"

"I didn't give it up. It was taken," Nye snapped. She looked away, biting her tongue to halt the words she wanted to hurl. She took a breath. "This is a very different situation. No one die—." She stopped herself again, frustrated that her mother had pushed her into talking about this. Struggling for control, she forced herself to continue more calmly. "I had to quit a job I didn't care about. I don't mind leaving KBA. I don't miss KBA. I will get a new job. I'm fine. All right?"

Her mother closed the refrigerator and picked up the paper grocery bag, now empty. She folded it, not looking at Nye.

Nye stifled a sigh and went to clear the table. She carried the plate and mug into the kitchen and walked around Jordan to set them in the sink. As she rinsed the mug, she wondered if she should say something to break the awkward silence.

"Your father and I have been thinking of another option."

Nye leaned back against the counter, facing her mother. She so disliked her mother's habit of saying "your father and I" anytime she wanted to present an idea she knew Nye wouldn't like. As if her father's involvement somehow lent more credibility to the idea. She crossed her arms. "Another option?"

"Yes." The shine of enthusiasm appeared in her mother's eyes. "Since you can't find a private equity position, why not get some use out of your other talents?"

Nye's apprehension grew as she sensed where this was leading.

"Now, I know you say you don't want to dance anymore."

Dance. She had said it. Nye couldn't believe even her mother would suggest dancing again.

"But what if you taught dance? You'd make a wonderful teacher, and I was thinking you could offer tango classes for

Oriana's kids." Her excitement seemed to block any perception of Nye's reaction as she continued. "Wouldn't that be wonderful? Those darling children need so much help, and I'm sure Oriana's employers would be happy to look at funding for a tango program. You could have a wonderful job, work with Oriana, you wouldn't have to move, and you could use your dance education—"

"Stop!" The word exploded with the cataclysm of emotion that had been building during the onslaught of painful suggestions.

Jordan whined softly as her mother raised hands to her chest.

Nye grappled for control. Even with all their problems, she had never spoken so sharply to her mother. She forced herself to breathe. "I thought I made it clear three years ago." She dropped her voice, but all her muscles were fraught with tension. "I will never dance or have anything to do with it ever again. That life is dead and nothing can ever change that. I am asking you to let it be … once and for all."

Their gazes locked in a battle of wills and determination.

The sound of the front door closing ended the face-off.

Jordan jogged out of the kitchen.

"Nye, are you around?" Oriana's cheerful presence swept into the room like sweet rain sent to wash away the blood on a battlefield. "Hi, Mom. I didn't know you were stopping by today."

Their mother smiled slightly, as she gathered her purse and the folded bag. "I just brought some food. I need to get going, though."

"Oh." Oriana watched her carefully. "Are you okay?"

Nye turned away from the sadness in her mother's face and puttered with a towel by the sink, trying not to feel guilty.

"Of course. I have to run."

Nye turned around in time to see her mother exit.

"Love you, girls. Bye."

"Bye, Mom. Love you, too!" Oriana called then turned to Nye.

"What?" Nye folded her arms across her chest. She couldn't help feeling defensive.

"Did something happen?"

Nye sighed and pushed away from the counter. "You know her." She passed Oriana and went into the living room, Jordan following closely behind. She glanced back at her sister, who stood in the open doorway. "She won't stop pushing."

"She's worried about you."

"I know." Nye sank onto the couch and rested a hand on Jordan's neck as he sat in front of her. "But she brought up dancing."

Oriana walked closer to where her sister sat. "What did she say?"

"She wants me to teach tango to your kids."

"Really?" Oriana raised her eyebrows. "That's a good idea."

Nye shot a glare at her sister. "Oriana!"

She held up a calming hand. "I just said it was a good idea, but it wasn't my idea. I wouldn't have brought it up."

Nye relaxed a little.

Oriana sat in the plush chair opposite the couch. "She just wants you to be happy."

"She wants me to dance," Nye corrected her. "She and Dad were never okay with my decision to quit tango."

"They knew how much you loved it."

"No, they didn't." Nye met Oriana's gaze. "If they had known, Mother wouldn't be comparing this situation to what happened three years ago."

"What do you mean?"

"She's afraid I'm going to move away or make some sort of drastic change." Nye lifted her feet as Jordan lowered himself down, squeezing his large frame between the couch and the coffee table. Nye rested her feet on his back. "She keeps acting like I'm going to go to pieces because I lost my job."

Oriana shrugged and looked slightly uncomfortable. "Losing a job is a serious thing for anyone. It can really shake a person up."

Nye narrowed her eyes. "Wait, why are you here right now?"

Oriana glanced away. "What do you mean?"

"You're not usually home during the day. What gives?"

"It's my lunch break."

Nye stared at Oriana, not letting her off the hook.

"Fine." Oriana met Nye's gaze, folding her arms in front of her. "I wanted to see how you were doing."

Nye groaned. "Not you, too."

"We only worry because we love you."

Nye leaned forward and met her sister's gaze. "Oriana, I'm fine. Really. I didn't care about my work at KBA. You should know that better than anyone. You're the one who was always telling me that I should get a job I enjoyed more."

"Yeah, but—"

"No, that's what I'm saying. I wasn't attached to my work, I didn't have friends there. I had nothing there that I can't lose." Nye's satisfaction with her detachment swelled as she listed the facts.

"What about Cullen?"

The question was like a needle jabbed through Nye's balloon of contentment. Of course, Oriana would manage to hit Nye's weak spot. She swallowed and responded with a calm she didn't feel. "What about him?"

"Can you lose him?"

Nye leaned back, avoiding Oriana's searching gaze.

"I never had him. I told you there couldn't be anything between us."

"Have you talked to him at all?"

"Not since I told him about Russell." Nye hated the sinking feeling in her stomach that accompanied the answer. She despised the fact that she cared at all, that she missed him. Yes, she had to admit she missed him, but only to herself. She would die before she'd say it to anyone else.

"You don't blame him, do you?"

Did she? Dan was really the one responsible for KBA's collapse, not Cullen. But the rollercoaster ride her life seemed to be turning into had started when the handsome lawyer showed up. She had been fine until Cullen. Yet here she was, almost a week since she had called him about his grandfather, and despite knowing it would be better if she never heard from him again, she caught herself holding her breath when the phone rang, hoping to hear his voice. Even when she woke from nightmares, her mind inevitably went to Cullen. She wondered what he was doing, if he thought of her at all and what he thought of her, if she'd ever see him again.

His presence was undoubtedly the reason her nightmares returned, and she had hoped that not seeing him anymore would return her emotions to their dormant state. The problem was, though she didn't see him face-to-face, she still saw him in her mind. The memories of his ice-melting grin, his deep chuckle, and even his pained expression when she last saw him were constantly with her. She thought about him even more than she thought about Dante. That was completely unacceptable … and terrifying.

"Nye." Oriana broke through Nye's contemplation. "What are you going to do if he calls?"

If only her sister would give up. "He won't."

"What makes you so sure?"

"I doubt he thinks well of me after what happened." It shouldn't bother her that his opinion about her would have changed, but it did.

"Why not? You didn't do anything."

"He overheard me talking with Dan and saw us together … He misunderstood." Partially. She didn't have a relationship with Dan, but Cullen probably also heard that she hadn't really answered Dan's plea to cover up his fraud.

"I'm sure you can clear it up, whatever happened. Just talk to him."

"It's none of my business what he thinks." Nye scooted to the end of the couch past Jordan and stood. "I need to get back to the job search. I'm going to check the listings online."

"Okay." Oriana sounded innocent, but Nye knew her sister wasn't fooled.

Oriana rose and headed for the door. "Oh," she stopped and turned back, "I almost forgot. Marcie said some guy called for you at school yesterday after I left."

"At Lincoln? Who was it?"

She shrugged. "I thought it might be Cullen at first, but he didn't give his name. I guess he asked if I worked there, if I was your sister, and then he wanted your phone number. Marcie said she didn't feel comfortable giving it to him, so she told him to call back. Made me glad our home number's unlisted."

Nye stared at Oriana, apprehension beginning to stir in her stomach.

"Nye? Are you okay?"

Nye blinked and tried to shake off her trepidation. "Yeah. Sure."

Oriana watched her closely. "You think it's someone you used to know? One of your friends?"

"No." That was exactly what she thought, but it couldn't be. It had been easy for Nye to cut off contact with her fellow dancers and acquaintances when Dante died. They had been more his friends than hers. Dante had been the only friend she ever needed.

"Oh my," Oriana said.

Nye glanced up. "What?"

"I didn't think anything of it before, but Marcie said the caller had a foreign accent."

Nye swallowed, the uneasiness curdling all the more, making her feel ill.

"You don't think it could be Nicanor? You said he had an accent, right?"

Nye nodded, her mind swirling with excuses to calm her anxiety. It couldn't be him. She had made it perfectly clear to Dante's closest friend that she never wanted to see him again. She refused to even imagine what would happen if she did. No. He wouldn't dare seek her out. It could not be him.

Suppressing her apprehension, she looked at her sister. "Don't worry about it, Oriana. I'm sure it's someone else."

"Really?" Oriana bit her lip.

"Absolutely positive." Nye felt more assured herself as she calmed Oriana's misgivings. All Nye's recent troubles were causing her imagination to run away with her. She needed to return to her old rational and realistic self. "Trust me. I know it isn't him, okay?"

Oriana's searching gaze must have found what she was looking for on Nye's face, because she nodded. "Okay." She headed for the door.

"Where are you going?"

Oriana turned to give Nye a questioning look. "To work."

Nye raised an eyebrow. "What about lunch?"

"Oh." Oriana flashed a mischievous grin. "I just ate with the kids."

Nye smiled in spite of herself, pleased to see the characteristic sparkle return to her sister's eyes. She waved Oriana away. "You are one of the kids."

Oriana scrunched up her nose at Nye and grabbed her coat. "Enjoy being lazy. Some of us have work to do." She dashed out the door, as Nye, to her own surprise, actually laughed.

A new wave of exhaustion swept over Cullen as another e-mail came through. He paused in his review of the contract for his grandfather's property, lifting sagging eyelids to check the new message on the computer. It was from Blanchard, giving Cullen another assignment to finish by tomorrow morning. Of course.

Cullen grabbed the mug off his desk and lifted it to his mouth. No energizing liquid touched his lips. He looked inside the empty mug and set it aside. Maybe it didn't matter; the office coffee was famously weak anyway, palatable only to the desperate souls forced to spend all night there.

He leaned his elbows on the desk and rested his heavy head in his hands. He had been drowning under a horrendous workload all week, and tonight he felt like he had taken his last breath before getting yanked under to stay. He was happy his grandfather had seen reason and allowed Cullen to look over offers made on the ranch, but the timing of the extra work couldn't be worse.

He had already reviewed two contracts for the land this week. Both of those turned out to be for casino development, though the buyers had led his grandfather to believe otherwise. The contract Cullen had been going over in detail for the last two hours looked more promising. It was a good offer, and the buyers wanted the land to build a shopping center. At least one thing might turn out well tonight.

Cullen ground his fingers into his already rumpled hair, wishing a solution for his other problem would present itself. His crushing caseload and the work for his grandfather only marked momentary reprieves from his emotional seesaw over Nye. In the days since her phone call, he had longed to talk to her again. He had reached for his cell phone countless times, only to pull back. He didn't have an excuse this time, no reason to call—nothing to make her want to even talk to the guy who had ruined her life, let alone say yes to a relationship.

He leaned back in the chair and stared at the phone lying on his desk. It wasn't like him to be afraid of rejection. Then again, most of what he had been going through since he met Nye was completely new. He didn't even get much pleasure out of the rare moments at his apartment that he used to treasure, because the abode that used to feel peaceful now seemed empty and oppressively silent. Before he met Nye, he had enjoyed the quiet independence of the single life and never really thought much about getting married or having a family. Now, he felt a loneliness that could only be explained by his burning desire to pursue a relationship with Nye.

Frightened by the change and the strength of his feelings for her, he had tried to use this time of separation to more actively seek God's will. He had to consider that the way the

KBA mess had turned out could be God's way of sending a message to Cullen that he didn't want to hear.

Was that it? Cullen looked up at the dark ceiling, starting to pray. *Should I let her go, Lord?* Call him crazy, and maybe Grant would, but the conviction that Cullen had about Nye stirred deep within. *She needs you.* Whether God whispered the words directly into Cullen's ear or just placed them on his heart, he couldn't be certain. But he did know one thing: God didn't want him to give up on Nye. He had some role yet that he was to play in her life. He only hoped that God also planned for Nye to fill the new hole in his own heart.

Riding on the assurance that he was following God's plan, Cullen grabbed the phone and started to dial. At the very least, calling her might unburden his mind long enough for him to get some work done.

"Chandler."

Cullen started and glanced up.

Blanchard stood in the doorway, glowering.

Cullen quickly slipped the phone in his pants pocket, feeling like his mom had just caught him stealing cookies.

"Don't let me interrupt." Blanchard's voice dripped with sarcasm.

"No problem." Cullen tried to maintain a calm façade, as his mind raced to figure out why Blanchard was upset.

The scowling partner walked into the office and gripped the back of a chair that faced Cullen's desk. He leaned forward in an intimidating pose. "Where's the Concord merger agreement?"

Cullen blinked. The agreement was one of the many he had to tackle yet tonight. "I'm working on it, sir. I thought you didn't need it until tomorrow."

Blanchard's cheeks flushed beet red. "And for me to have it in hand tomorrow morning, you would have to get it to me tonight, wouldn't you?"

Cullen chafed under the caustic question. He was usually hard to rile, but something about Blanchard seemed to bring out the worst in him. Restraining his irritation, Cullen responded with civility. "I'm trying my best, but I'm working on a deal with Mr. Fletcher that's closing tomorrow, and, of course, the two purchase agreements for you." Cullen hoped the reminder that he was working on projects with other partners, like Fletcher, might help Blanchard add more realism to his expectations.

"I'm not surprised you can't handle your workload, when you're spending your time and this office's resources on personal affairs."

Cullen stared, stunned by the allegation. What was he even talking about?

"Your relatives are not clients of this firm, and unless they wish to pay for the privilege, any legal assistance you provide must be done on your own time."

Cullen was flabbergasted. Blanchard must be talking about Cullen's grandfather, but how had the overbearing partner even found out that Cullen was reviewing those offers? He must have gotten wind of the research tasks Cullen had asked his assistant to perform in order to find out more about the buyers interested in the land. Cullen hadn't thought that was wrong to do—the cursory research only took Sarah a few minutes.

Cullen opened his mouth to respond, then closed it. He had no answer against the accusation, because Blanchard was right. The time Cullen spent reviewing offers on the ranch undeniably interfered with getting his work for the firm done as quickly as he otherwise could. And he was definitely not getting paid to assist his grandfather.

Blanchard's brows drew together in a concentrated look of disgust as he pulled himself to his full medium height. "Some of the other partners believed you to be on the fast-track to partnership when you arrived here. I must say your increasing disregard for the priorities of this firm has begun to persuade them otherwise." The displeasure on Blanchard's face lessened. "Even I must admit you have unusual skill as an attorney, and that is the only reason I'm warning you to improve now or face the consequences."

With his last words, Blanchard spun on his heel and headed for the door. "I want the Concord agreement in one hour." He didn't turn as he flung the order and marched out of the office.

Feeling like he had just survived a tidal wave, Cullen stared at the empty doorway. He put in so much work, dedicated so much time to this job, and it still wasn't enough. He had been able to keep up with his assignments until the situations with Nye and his grandfather were added to the mix.

Cullen didn't know what to do. How could he balance them all and still perform at work? Blended with Blanchard's warning had been an unexpected acknowledgement of Cullen's ability. Despite the sting of the reprimand, a part of Cullen treasured the affirmation of his potential. He couldn't allow everything he had worked for to be destroyed when he was finally getting close to reaping some rewards.

He closed the folder over the contract he had been studying. Reviewing offers for the ranch at the office was out of the question from now on. But with his caseload, he didn't have any personal time to use for the task. He didn't care how pressured he felt—he was not about to leave his grandfather in the lurch. His grandfather had already apologized for bothering Cullen and spoke worriedly about the strain on his grandson every time he reluctantly gave Cullen another contract to review. Far worse than admitting the truth of his grandfather's fears would be to leave him with no one to help him interpret offers at all. Cullen's grandfather was a highly intelligent man, but his formal education had been sporadic even at the high school level. He needed a lawyer or ... a businesswoman?

Cullen's pulse sped up as he thought of Nye. It just might work. His grandfather kept suggesting that she might have more time to help him. Had Cullen not been so enthralled with Nye himself, he might have been jealous of the affection his grandfather clearly had for her, even preferring her assistance over Cullen's.

For Cullen's part, he could relax if Nye were helping. Her business expertise made her perfectly qualified for the job, and he knew he could trust her. The fact that her life would once again become intertwined with his was an added bonus that he tried to convince himself was not the deciding factor. With the longed-for excuse to call Nye finally in hand, he again reached for his phone, this time with a silent prayer that she say yes.

Chapter Thirteen

*"There is a dance, and the greatest need of your life
is to get into that dance."*
–Dr. Timothy Keller

"I can't agree to this." Russell shook his head, as he sat across from Nye at the kitchen table, the contract clutched in his stiff fingers.

It had been easy for Nye to agree to fill in for Cullen. Despite all the warning bells ringing in her head, she had been happy to hear from him when he called, though she wished she could have hung on to more resentment or even guilt— anything to keep her more frightening feelings for him at bay.

Her effort at emotional distance had melted into compassion when she heard the desperation and fatigue in his voice. She knew what it was like to be under pressure from work, and she wanted to do all she could to lessen his burden.

It seemed like a win-win for Nye, anyway, since she had been surprised by how much she missed Russell. It was a joy to see him again, but if she had been able to anticipate the illogical stubbornness that overtook him at the sight of this contract, she might not have been so quick to volunteer.

"I'm afraid I still don't understand. This is a good offer. Cullen looked it over. I looked it over. They don't want to build a casino. What don't you like about it?"

"The shopping center."

She let out an unexpected sneeze.

He blinked, concern softening his gaze. "Gesundheit. Are you sick?"

"I don't think so." She waved away his concern and sniffed. She had been feeling a bit off all day, but she hoped the minor symptoms wouldn't turn into a full-blown illness.

"Sounds like a cold coming on. You should eat some chicken soup. Would you like some?"

"No, and don't try to change the subject." She gave him a firm look. "What's wrong with a shopping center?"

"I don't want shopping malls and great big stores here—greedy people bustling around, stomping over my ranch."

Exasperated, she leaned back in the chair and crossed her arms. "Then what do you want done with the land?"

"I wouldn't mind some little houses here. Quiet places where nice folks could settle, maybe raise their families."

Nye shook her head at the idyllic image. "I'm afraid that's impossible. Your land has been rezoned as commercial property. If anyone buys it from you, they have to use it for commercial purposes."

He tossed the contract onto the table. "Well, find me some buyers who want to build small businesses then. Little stores, shops … what do you call them?" He paused and looked away as if to find the term on the walls. "Privately owned. That's it." He turned back. "I want places like that, not some sprawling monstrosity."

She leaned forward and watched him until he met her gaze. "Russell, you can't limit the sale so much or no one will buy. The shopping center developers are willing to pay a lot to purchase your property right now. You need to start thinking about the deadline coming up. You only have one more week before you either need to sell or start on the property changes, which we both know you can't afford." She reached for his hand that rested on the table and gave it a gentle squeeze. "Take this offer while you can."

He stared at her hand on his. When he looked up, his eyes glistened with tears. "I can't do it. Not for that."

She didn't know what to say. She had thought he was only against casinos being built on his property. At least that objection had some plausible grounds for moral objections. She couldn't understand why he was so resistant to the idea of a shopping mall, but her frustration with his refusal vanished when she saw the emotion on his face. He usually seemed so matter-of-fact about selling that she was taken aback by the sadness in his eyes. She wasn't sure she understood the cause of it.

Not knowing what else to do, she just rested her hand on his, offering silent comfort and hoping he would soon see reason and make the right decision.

The gusting wind drove her back, as she strained to reach the water. Dark waves crashed over him. Her heart screamed. The waves pounded, pounded ...

A distant, pounding noise woke Nye from the dark dream. She tried to open her sleep-encrusted eyes.

A low rumble came from directly in front of her.

More pounding. Then the rumble led to a loud bark.

She sat up with a jerk. "Jordan, hush." Nothing like the deep voice of a hundred-pound dog to wake a person up.

Nye looked around the room from the couch, trying to get her bearings. She was at her house, in the living room. Through the muddled fog of her mind, she vaguely remembered feeling congested and tired when she got home from seeing Russell. She had started to read a book and must have fallen asleep. She looked at the clock above the fireplace. Six o'clock.

The pounding started again. This time, she could identify the noise as knocking at the front door.

Jordan, standing by the couch and watching the door, rumbled another low-pitched growl.

Nye rose to her feet and shuffled to the door, the jingle of Jordan's collar tags following her. As she walked, she pulled the elastic band from her hair and ran her hand through the tangled waves that fell past her shoulders.

She opened the door, and her heart stopped.

Cullen stood on the doorstep and flashed the grin that turned her brain to porridge even on a good day. "Hi."

Spoken in his deep, gentle tone, that one word was enough to send shivers up her spine.

"I'm here on a mission."

"A mission?" Her sleep-fogged mind couldn't begin to fathom what he was talking about.

"Yep. To heal the sick." He took in her expression, which likely appeared more than a little befuddled. "Granddad called me."

"He didn't." She wasn't sure whether to be touched or annoyed by the insistence that someone needed to take care of her.

"Afraid so. He wanted me to bring some chicken soup over, but I thought pizza sounded much better." Cullen tilted the box he was holding so she could see it was from a local pizzeria. "Hope you haven't eaten dinner yet." He looked down at Jordan, who watched him carefully from her side. "I didn't know you had a dog."

"Pizza for a cold?" She spotted a Scrabble box hidden underneath the pizza. "And Scrabble?"

"Haven't you heard of Scrabble's medicinal powers?" His grin turned sheepish under her skeptical gaze. "Okay, you got me. I can't pass up the chance to take advantage of an invalid. I brought my own in case you tried to get out of it by saying you don't have Scrabble." His eyes twinkled mischievously.

She stared at him, trying to take it all in.

He looked at her clothes and hair, and realization seemed to dawn. "Did I wake you?"

"Huh? Oh." She raised a hand to smooth her hair, suddenly aware of how awful she must look. Her blonde strands were falling wherever they wanted, fuzzy and mussed from sleep, and she was dressed in comfortable, but unflattering lounge clothes.

Cullen's gaze followed her hand's motion over her unkempt hair. He met her gaze, his eyes darkening. "You look beautiful," he said softly.

Her breath caught. She couldn't look away from the warmth in his eyes. In the back of her mind, those warning signals blared. She better not let him in the house. Her emotional defenses wouldn't stand a chance.

"So what do you say? Scrabble party? Consider it a thank you for helping Granddad."

She looked at him, battling between her desires and her better judgment.

"Or you could just leave me standing out in the snow with a cold pizza." A slow grin tugged at his mouth.

She struggled to hold back an answering smile, as she pretended to consider his question. "What's on it?"

"The pizza? Everything but anchovies."

"Well, in that case …" She laughed and gave in, backing away from the doorway. "Come on in." Score another point for that grin.

Taking her laughter as a sign of endorsement for the visitor, Jordan wagged his tail as Cullen entered.

"Hey there, big fella." Cullen stroked Jordan with his free hand.

"May I take your coat?

Cullen looked up. "Oh, sure."

"You can set your stuff there." She indicated a small table by the door.

"Thanks."

The coat he handed her was heavy and warm in her arms. She caught a whiff of pleasant cologne as she hung it on the rack. Honestly. His coat even smelled good.

"What's his name?"

She turned to see him petting his new friend. "Jordan."

Soaking up the attention, the huge shepherd leaned against Cullen's legs.

Cullen laughed and took a step back to balance himself against the dog's considerable weight. "Wow, he's big." Cullen glanced at Nye with a smile. "Great dog."

"I take it you like dogs?" She didn't know why that pleased her so much.

"Oh, yeah. Love 'em." He straightened from petting Jordan. "I'd have one if my landlord allowed it."

"I don't know what I'd do without Jordan to keep me company. Oriana's actually gone right now, so it's just the two of us here tonight."

"Oh. That's too bad." Something in Cullen's tone as he glanced away sounded less than convincing.

Her eyes narrowed as she watched him. "You already knew that, didn't you?"

He looked at her with humor in his dark gaze. "Oriana might've mentioned she goes to Bible study Friday nights."

"I see." This time, she didn't try to stop the smile that crept onto her face.

He grabbed the game and pizza off the table. "So where do you want to eat?"

She let him change the subject, not sure she had the courage to address the planning he had put into this. "Living room's fine." She gestured to the open room where the two couches flanked a coffee table near the lit fireplace.

He headed for the table and glanced back. "This okay?" He indicated that he would set the pizza and Scrabble on the coffee table.

"Sure." She watched him, entranced by the way his presence filled the house.

He straightened and caught her staring.

She turned away. "I'll get some plates for the pizza." She headed for the kitchen.

"Let me help," he offered as he followed her. "So how are you feeling? Very sick?"

"I feel much better after my nap. I think I'm beating ..." Her voice trailed off as she turned to Cullen and found him dangerously close. Ordinarily, she thought their kitchen was quite spacious, but the room seemed to have shrunk to half its usual size. She tried to calm the tingling of her senses and gathered her thoughts to finish the sentence. "... Beating the virus or whatever it is." She pointed to a cabinet door near the corner. "The plates are in there." She breathed again when he moved away to open it.

"I'll get the napkins." She crouched down to locate the paper napkins in a cabinet under the counter, glad for the distraction of doing something. What had she been thinking? She couldn't even get within three feet of this man without her heart going into a tailspin. How could she manage to keep her emotional guard up when she was alone with him for the evening?

She tried to push past the Cullen-charmed confusion of her mind to remember why it was essential that she protect herself. She hadn't gotten hurt when she lost her job because her survival plan worked. No attachments. And absolutely no romantic relationships. She understood better than anyone that the potential pain was not worth the risk. With that little mental pep talk, she grabbed a wad of napkins and stood, turning to face the trouble she'd created for herself.

"Are these okay?" Cullen held out two plates like a little boy awaiting approval.

Her heart lurched. If only this particular trouble were not so endearing, she might stand a fighting chance.

Nye laughed, disarmed by another of Cullen's teasing quips. They sat on the floor on opposite sides of the coffee table, locked in their second Scrabble match in two hours. In the midst of the competition, she was surprised to realize how relaxed she was. Maybe she was just getting too tired to fight her feelings for Cullen, or perhaps his charm was too strong to resist for long. Either way, any struggle on her part seemed pointless as his intelligent conversation and easy-going humor chipped away at her defenses.

She added two letters to a word on the board and smiled.

"No, way." His eyes widened in horror, but their twinkle gave him away. "Man, your sister wasn't kidding. You really are a wicked Scrabble player."

She laughed again. "You're not exactly rolling over either."

"Not yet anyway."

"Must be a family trait."

He gave her a questioning glance.

"Stubbornness, never giving up on a point."

"You mean Granddad." Cullen shook his head. "I can't believe he won't sell because of a shopping center. I really don't understand it any more than you do. It's not like him to be unreasonable." Cullen leaned back, meeting her gaze. "I wish I could do something about it, but there's not much hope of that if his mind's made up. My grandmother was the only one who could ever get him to change his mind when he was set on something."

"I reminded him that he doesn't have much time. I'm hoping he'll think about it and come around."

As Cullen watched her, his mouth angled into a smile. "I'm guessing he won't be able to resist your persuasion for long. He seems quite taken with you."

A blush heated her face. "If you're trying to throw me off my game, it won't work." She pointed to the Scrabble board. "It's your turn."

Her distraction tactic succeeded, and he mercifully looked away. A smile on her lips, she watched his brow furrow as he concentrated on his lettered pieces. If this was a defeat of her emotional defenses, it was the sweetest loss she'd ever tasted.

Over the pizza and Scrabble, she was reminded of how easy it was to talk to Cullen. Like the afternoon at church, conversation flowed naturally as they discovered how much they had in common. They shared an enjoyment of chocolate desserts, coffee, tennis, winter, and snow. They liked the same movies and, of course, pizzas with everything but anchovies and Scrabble. Not only did their tastes and interests match, but she was starting to realize that their minds and personalities seemed to be made for each other.

"So what about your family?" Cullen suddenly asked.

She came out of her reverie and looked at the board. "Did you take your turn already?"

"No, I'm still thinking. But before you distracted me, we were talking about my family. Now I want to hear about yours."

"I didn't distract you. It was the other way around. And I still wasn't done asking about your family."

He smiled and fiddled with his letters, looking at the board. "Okay, shoot."

"Did your brother ever resent you? When he was getting into trouble and you weren't? I bet your parents probably doted on you then."

His smile faded, and he looked at her with a thoughtful gaze. "Chase resented almost everyone when he was a teenager. At least, that's how he acted and what he said. He tried to push me away a lot. He'd trash my stuff, blow me off when I wanted to do things with him. We had a small house at the time and shared a room. That was rough, but I think it was good, too. It forced us to be close even when we didn't want to be, you know? I think it made it easier to go back to being friends when he eventually turned around. But as far as my parents were concerned, they actually ended up spending more time on Chase than me because of his problems. He demanded the attention, I guess."

"Did that bother you?" Could he possibly relate to her feeling that her parents preferred Oriana and approved of her while they so clearly disapproved of their eldest child? Nye doubted that would be the case with Cullen's now-perfect Christian family.

"Maybe subconsciously sometimes. I don't know. I tried as hard as I could to do really well in school and stay out of trouble. I guess I just wanted everything to be okay again. But it didn't get better until Chase came to the Lord."

The natural way he spoke about God somehow lessened Nye's usual antagonistic reaction. She was even a little curious. "Why wasn't he a Christian already? Your parents were, right?"

He shook his head. "Not when we were little. Mom and Dad both became Christians at a Bible study our neighbor invited them to. That was the year my brother turned fifteen." Cullen smiled. "He didn't exactly like the changes at our house when Mom and Dad got 'religious,' as he put it."

"What did you think?" She watched him, intent on his answer.

"I didn't really care. Pretty much went along with the changes and even started going to church with them. I went through the motions of accepting everything my parents believed at the time, but I didn't get serious about a personal commitment to Christ until I went to college." He looked at her as she digested the surprising information.

"And everything's better now?"

"Well, it isn't perfect, of course. But we're a very close family. My brother and I are good friends, and my parents are terrific. My dad is an amazing guy—I can always go to him for advice." He grinned. "And my mom calls me at least twice a week."

"Checking up on you?"

"Only when I need it." He winked.

Her pulse surged in response to the gesture. She was envious of the love in his eyes as he spoke of his family. Despite a troubled history, he still seemed to have the kind of doting, affectionate parents that Nye's father and mother had ceased to be when she left her dancing career.

"What about you?"

Buying time, she took the evasive route. "What about me?"

"You're close to Oriana, that's obvious, but what about your parents? Do you have a good relationship with them? Or are you going to keep avoiding the question?" He raised an eyebrow, the corner of his mouth twitching with amusement.

He was treading on precarious ground, but to Nye's surprise, her defenses didn't go up. She didn't even tense. Looking into his dark, understanding gaze, she felt a stirring desire to confide in him, if only a little.

She took a breath. "We used to be close. Our whole family was the way yours sounds like now. We were affectionate with each other, really supportive. We had little ups and downs, but nothing serious. My parents were Christians before they got married, and they raised us going to church and everything. Then ..."

She licked her lips and glanced away. What had she gotten herself into? She wasn't sure how to explain further without revealing much more than she was prepared to tell. Without intending to, she met his gaze and was calmed by the interested understanding she saw in his eyes. "Things happened after I graduated, and we drifted apart. You're right. Oriana and I are still good friends, but my parents are ... We don't really understand each other anymore."

"I'm sorry. That has to be hard."

She looked away from the compassion in his eyes.

"I know it took quite a while for my brother to patch things up with our parents. They pretty much had to start from scratch and build a whole new relationship."

Nye cleared her throat, not sure how he had gotten her to talk about that topic. "I think you're setting some kind of turn record here." She gave him what she hoped was a bright smile.

"Okay, okay. I'll concentrate," he said, good-humoredly, and went back to studying his letter pieces.

She was grateful that he took the hint and let her change

the subject. Somehow she could not give Cullen the evasive, pat answers she usually used to field personal questions. The urge she felt to confide in him was dangerous to say the least. It was another power he possessed that made her vulnerable. And yet, she felt a little better from having shared something so personal with him. He understood, and she liked him all the more for that. As long as they stayed away from any detailed discussion of her past, everything would be fine.

"Ah-ha!" Cullen placed letters following the "T" of a word already on the board.

Her throat went dry as she read the word: tango.

He glanced at her with a guileless smile. "Not very impressive, I know, but I'll take what I can get."

She tore her gaze from the board and tried to force a smile, hoping he wouldn't notice her distress.

"Nye?" His eyes darkened as he watched her.

She wished she could get her hands on whoever started the story that men weren't sensitive to women's emotions.

"What is it? Why does dance bother you so much?"

Summoning up her courage, she tried for an innocent expression. "Bother me?" She glanced away. "I don't know what you mean." She stroked Jordan, who lay beside her.

"I've seen the way you look every time I ask about your dancing career, about tango. Now just the word is enough to make you turn white."

She swallowed, tension returning in full force.

"It's like you're afraid of it."

She met his searching gaze with her steady one. "I'm really not sure what you're getting at. Dancing isn't something I talk about a lot, but I certainly don't have a problem with it." The lie lodged like a cancerous lump in her throat. Why did she deny it? It was easy to refuse to talk about the past with her family, but, somehow, revealing such a private issue to Cullen seemed like admitting a weakness. Weak or not, it was survival. If she confessed she didn't want to talk about dance, she would have to explain why, and that was out of the question.

He watched her with an expression she couldn't read. "So you're perfectly fine with dance?"

"Of course." She hoped she sounded nonchalant as she looked away, again petting Jordan as an excuse. She could tell by Cullen's tone that he didn't believe her at all, and she braced herself, certain he would use the opportunity to drill her about her past.

"Okay. Let's dance."

Nye's breath whooshed out of her lungs. Her gaze swung to his face.

He watched her, gauging her reaction.

"When?"

"Right now. You have a nice stereo system here." He abruptly stood and went to the cabinet that housed the system she shared with Oriana. "Any good music?"

"What? I don't know." She floundered for a coherent answer. He was moving too fast, and she couldn't form a defensive plan quickly enough. "I don't ... Oriana uses it more than I do." The understatement was a floundering attempt to disguise another circumstance she couldn't explain.

For as long as she could remember, Nye had never just listened to music—she felt it. The sounds filled her being, seeping into her soul until she had to move with the expressions of the music. She couldn't sever her passion for dancing from music when Dante was alive, and she hadn't been able to separate the two after his death. Music embodied what she had lost and made her long for something that had to stay in the past. It was tied to the person she was then, the woman who had died with Dante.

"Here we are." Cullen selected something on the mp3 player connected to the system. "This should do it."

The strains of a romantic ballad flowed out of the speakers and filled the room. Lost in the strange experience of hearing music in her home, Nye didn't notice him approach.

"May I have this dance?" The deep voice came from directly above, and Cullen's outstretched hand appeared in front of her.

She looked up at him. "I ... Are you sure you want to do this?"

"Of course. I like dancing. Unless you don't want to for some reason?" He let the question hang, the hint of a challenge in his gaze.

She stared at his hand. Where was that inner strength she relied upon? Of course she could handle one dance. Annoyed that she doubted herself so much, she placed her hand in his. She immediately regretted the action as he helped her to her feet, and she became acutely aware of how perfectly her hand fit into his, as if covered in a cocoon of warmth and safety. But she wasn't safe at all.

The danger increased when he slowly pulled her closer, and her breathing grew ragged with the proximity. She tried not to think about the feel of his strong arm on her back, as she hesitantly rested her hand on the taut muscles of his shoulder. She couldn't meet his gaze.

He started to sway with the music, beginning with a basic box step. As she followed his lead, her instincts and years of training took over. She pressed closer to him as they left the box step behind, spinning, turning as one. Nye forgot where she was, forgot everything but the feel of dancing to the strains of the orchestra.

She was swept away, dancing with Dante in an empty studio, or at a beach, or a field, or in the clouds. She couldn't tell where she was, but she was happy. Joy welled up within, filling empty crevices that had long been cold and dormant.

This was good. This was right. Held in Dante's arms as he

led her beautifully through the dance, communicating his next move by the slight pressure of his hand on her back, Nye felt complete.

He pulled her even closer, slowing until they stopped. She raised her head as he lowered his, and their lips met in a tender kiss.

Cullen. The dream vanished. It wasn't Dante who held her in his arms, it was Cullen. But the pleasure of the kiss locked her in the embrace, and she followed her instincts to respond.

The music stopped. In the silence, horror at what she was doing flooded her conscience.

She pushed him away, barely registering his stunned expression as her thoughts whirled. How could she have gotten so confused? How could she have danced with another man? Kissed another man? The heart she didn't know she still had, warmed for a brief moment, was ripped from her chest, leaving a searing wound. The pain from her betrayal of Dante and the reminder of what she had lost made her long for the cold ache she knew so well.

"Nye, what is it? What's wrong?" Cullen reached for her.

She jerked away, staring blankly at the flames in the fireplace. She vaguely registered the start of the next song on the player.

"Please tell me. Let me help you." His voice sounded distant and faint, prodding at her through the throb.

"Just go." Her words came out as a weak whisper.

He stepped closer. "Nye, I can help … if you'll just let me in."

"No."

"What?"

Nye mustered her strength and looked at him. "You need to leave. Now."

Hurt filled his eyes.

"Please." She turned away, unable to face his pain as well as hers. She didn't watch, only listened as he took his coat and left. The front door clicked behind him. She closed her eyes.

If only she could dismiss her pain the same way. She wanted to shut out the reality that dancing still touched her soul like nothing else, to banish the fact that she had enjoyed Cullen's kiss, had yearned to respond even when she knew he wasn't Dante. And she desperately wanted to dispel the most terrifying realization of all—she was falling in love with Cullen.

Chapter Fourteen

"To everything there is a season,
A time for every purpose under heaven ...
A time to mourn,
And a time to dance."
–Ecclesiastes 3:1, 4

"You what?"

Nye winced inwardly at Oriana's shocked question as she looked out the passenger window of her sister's car, staring blankly at snow-covered houses as they passed.

"A guy shows up with pizza and your favorite game," Oriana continued from behind the wheel, "and you tell him to get lost because he wants to dance with you? Some women would kill for that kind of romance."

Nye swallowed. She couldn't think of a thing to say in her own defense.

"I'm sorry." Oriana sighed. "I'm not being very helpful, am I?"

Nye turned her head forward. "No, you're right. I shouldn't have told him to leave. I guess I panicked. Couldn't think straight. The music, the dancing, it was like a dream—"

Oriana reached for Nye's hand and gave it a comforting squeeze. "I know. You don't have to explain."

"I wish I could explain. I wish I knew what to do."

Oriana returned her hand to the steering wheel to guide the car through a turn. "Was it a good dream or a bad dream?"

Nye looked out the window again. The yards they passed, blanketed in sheets of white, turned a surreal blue under the moonlight of early evening. "I don't even know that. It was wonderful at first, even when he kissed me—"

"He kissed you?"

Nye closed her eyes against the memory, still so vivid though a day had passed. She nodded.

"Do you like him, Nye? I mean really like him?"

Nye looked down at her hands, which she was unconsciously twisting together. They were cold, clammy. "I'm afraid I might."

"Not good enough."

Nye had rarely heard her sister sound so serious.

"You have to decide how you feel and what you're going to do about it. You can't go on like this, dragging him along while you try to make up your mind. It's not fair to him, and it's not fair to you."

She opened her mouth to respond, then closed it. Was that really what she had been doing? She thought a moment. "I didn't mean to do that. I don't want to hurt him."

Oriana turned the car onto the street where their parents lived. "I know, but you're doing it anyway."

Nye wanted to deny it. Her instinct was to argue that Cullen didn't care for her enough to be hurt, but she had seen the look in his eyes when she'd pushed him away. Her sister was right.

Oriana brought the car to a stop along the curb in front of their parents' house and turned to Nye. "Well, here we are."

Nye stared at the one-story, brick house. It wasn't the home she had grown up in. Her parents had sold their large, old house in the quiet outskirts of Harper and moved closer to downtown after their daughters left home. Given the problems Nye had started having with her parents in recent years, she didn't have many positive associations with their new house. This evening, it looked appropriately dark and uninviting under trees that blocked the moon's rays. "I'm really not up to this tonight."

"It's their anniversary, Nye. We have to go."

Nye sighed and opened the car door. She stepped into the frigid air and belted her coat as she waited for Oriana to retrieve the wrapped gift from the backseat. Oriana closed the door and they started up the narrow, shoveled sidewalk that led to the front door.

"I don't know how you do it." Nye glanced at her sister as they walked.

"What?"

"You always get up for these things. Even talk me into going."

Oriana shrugged. "You know it's not as hard for me. They don't … act the same with me as they do with you."

"You mean they don't put you through the wringer every time they see you." Nye couldn't help a small smile. "The sky isn't going to fall if you say something critical about them, you know."

"Hey, it might." Oriana laughed and threw her free arm around Nye's shoulders. "And who knows, you might have fun tonight."

Nye grimaced as they reached the house and stopped in front of the door.

Oriana lowered her voice to a conspiratorial whisper. "Here's the plan: I'll distract Mom, and you grab the cheesecake."

Surprised by the joke, Nye let out a spontaneous burst of laughter that made her feel one hundred times better. What would she do without Oriana?

Before they could knock, the door swung open. Their mother stood in the entry, staring at Nye.

"Happy anniversary!" Oriana's smile beamed with enthusiasm.

Recovering from her surprise, their mother smiled warmly. "Welcome, girls. I'm so glad you could both make it."

"Happy anniversary." Nye's greeting was decidedly less energetic than her sister's as she followed Oriana inside, her amusement having completely dissipated. She supposed it should be disturbing that her mother was shocked to see her laugh, but the prospect of the evening ahead was too dire for her to worry about anything else.

A few weeks ago, when Mother had asked Oriana and Nye if they'd be free for a dinner to celebrate their parents' thirtieth anniversary, Nye had thought, or perhaps hoped, she'd have too much work. She had said she would try to fit it in, but secretly planned to use busyness with the Sheffield deal as an excuse to avoid an evening of censure with her parents. Now she was robbed of that reasonable pretext, and her determined sister had refused to help her create one. Oriana had instead used her considerable persuasive powers to convince Nye that she had to go to the dinner.

As Nye unbuttoned her coat in the warm house, she became aware that the situation would be even worse than she had imagined all those weeks ago. Instead of criticizing Nye's work habits or referencing her past with disapproval, her mother might push the idea of teaching dance, or she could even talk about Cullen. Nye shuddered at the thought.

"I can take your coat, honey," Mother said from behind her.

"Thanks."

She took Nye's coat and hung it on a nearby rack.

"Need any help with dinner?" Oriana asked.

"It's almost ready, but I'm sure there's some job I can give you."

Nye couldn't help but notice that the smile their mother bestowed on Oriana held no judgment, no dissatisfaction.

"Nye," the pleased glow faded as she looked at her other daughter, "will you track down your father and tell him dinner's almost ready? He was showing the pool table to our company, and you know what he's like with pool. He'll be in there for hours."

"Oh, you invited someone else?" Oriana followed their mother to the kitchen.

Nye sighed, relieved for the moment. At least she had gained a little space. She passed the living room and headed for her father's study. After his retirement a year ago, Dad had removed his desk from the study and replaced it with a pool table—his pride and joy. Nye wasn't surprised he was showing it to their guests.

As she neared the study, Nye heard the murmur of voices. They stopped as she reached the open doorway. She peered into the dimly lit room, vaguely registering a tall figure out of the corner of her eye as she spotted her father.

He held a cue stick in his hand and beamed a smile at her. "You're finally here. Good, we can eat."

Nye smiled at the teasing. "Happy anniversary, anyway. I'm supposed to …" Her voice trailed off when her gaze, adjusting to the darkness, moved to the other guest, and she saw the handsome face that had been tormenting her since the evening before.

She had expected a friend of her parents' from church, some unknown newcomer, or even the pastor himself—anyone but Cullen. She tried to recover from her shock and read his expression. No good. From the far side of the pool table, his eyes glinted with something she couldn't interpret in the shadows of the room. Was he angry? Her nerves tensed. She wished she could see him better or that he would say something.

Her father cleared his throat. "I believe you two already know each other?"

Nye jerked to look at him, startled he was there. His eyes held a glimmer of amusement as he watched her.

"We do." Cullen's tone was as serious as his gaze.

Nye threw a warning glance at her father, hoping he wouldn't make more out of the situation.

"What did your mother want?" he asked, mercifully taking the hint.

"Dinner's almost ready."

"Great. We'll be right there. Just a few more balls to go." Her father moved around the table to eye up a shot.

Nye's gaze was drawn irresistibly back to Cullen. She hadn't noticed before that he also held a cue stick.

He still watched her, pinning her with that unreadable expression.

She couldn't move.

"Your turn, Cullen," her father said.

He slowly looked away and surveyed the table.

She seized the opportunity and made a quick exit, feeling every inch a coward. Better to live to fight another day.

As she headed for the dining room, Nye tried to calm the frustration building up inside. She didn't have to be a genius to know her mother was the one who thought inviting Cullen was a good idea—no doubt intentionally to make sure that he and Nye would have to see each other.

Nye needed time and space to sort out her feelings for Cullen. Thanks to her mother's wayward matchmaking attempts, she wasn't going to get either. Panic rose above her frustration. She couldn't do it. She couldn't sit across from him and make conversation, acting like nothing had happened.

She reached the entryway and stopped, staring at her coat. She could leave. Plead a headache or some illness when they asked. Oriana would understand.

"Nye?" her mother called from the kitchen.

Nye stepped toward her coat, almost reaching for it.

"Oh, there you are." Mother approached, carrying a spoon. "Did you tell your father?"

Nye nodded. "They're almost done."

"Let's hope that means he won't play another game before they come to dinner." She smiled. "You saw Cullen?"

Nye took in her mother's hopeful expression. "I saw him."

"Good." Her mother pressed her lips together, a sure sign she was trying to resist saying more. "Why don't you come and help get the food on the table?"

"Sure." Nye followed her to the kitchen where Oriana emerged carrying their mother's favorite covered platter.

Oriana glanced at their mother to be sure her back was turned before giving Nye a sympathetic look. "I didn't know," she whispered.

"It's okay," Nye murmured. It wasn't, but there was no reason for Oriana to feel bad about it. Nye entered the kitchen with the angst of a sentenced prisoner about to face the gallows. She had missed her chance for escape, and the dinner she expected to be unpleasant had just become impossible.

Cullen was sitting across from the woman of his dreams, and she couldn't look more miserable. In fact, she looked downright ill. He glanced at the rest of the family seated around the table, whose furtive glances at each other betrayed that they knew something was wrong.

"So, Cullen, I hear you're the reason our daughter's out of a job?"

Cullen shot Marcus a startled glance, as Nye sputtered and coughed. Thankful he hadn't been in the middle of swallowing food himself, Cullen hesitated as he tried to determine if Marcus was joking. After playing pool with him for half an hour, Cullen was learning that though Nye had inherited her blonde hair and blue-eyed beauty from her mother, her personality was closer to her father's. In Marcus, however, the calm, serious demeanor that characterized his eldest daughter was sprinkled heavily with a sarcastic sense of humor that Cullen had glimpsed only rarely in Nye.

"Marcus," Caroline chided.

At the head of the table, Marcus looked up from his plate with a twinkle in his eyes.

Relieved, Cullen smiled weakly. "I guess you could say that, sir—though that certainly wasn't my intention." He snuck a glance at Nye.

She was taking a long drink of water, her face flushed. At least it was a change from the pale white her complexion had been since she spotted him by the pool table.

"From what I've heard," Marcus continued, "we should probably thank you. Did you ever find out how much that Akkerman fellow stole?"

"Not an exact figure, no."

"Well, I hope the authorities recovered all of it. It's hard to believe Nye's employer would be the kind of man who—"

"Does it really matter?" Nye shot Marcus an irritated look.

"Yes, it does. Not many fathers get to find out their daughters work for criminals. You remember I was never thrilled about you working there."

"Oh, I remember." Nye's blue eyes flashed.

Was she that angry for herself or because she still had feelings for Dan? Cullen wished he knew.

"So, Cullen," Caroline jumped in, covering the awkwardness with a beaming smile. "You must miss your family, being so far away. Do you hear from them often?"

Cullen pulled his gaze away from Nye. "I talk with my brother now and then, and my mother calls a lot."

"A woman after my own heart." Caroline's eyes, so like Nye's, sparkled.

"Did you get to see them over the holidays?" Oriana, seated next to Nye, piped up with the question. Even Oriana's characteristic energy was being dimmed by the tension of the dinner.

"I did. My parents came here for Thanksgiving, and I managed to go home for Christmas." The reminder of those visits did little to improve Cullen's frame of mind. He only had a short time to spend with his family during the holidays because of needing to get back to work. His family had been kind enough not to say anything when he barely saw them at Thanksgiving and was only home for Christmas Day, but he had felt the disappointment they didn't voice. He hoped he wouldn't have such ill-timed projects to finish during the holiday season next winter.

"That must've been nice. I can't imagine living that far away from family." Oriana cast an awkward glance at her family members, seeming to realize the irony of her statement at such a time.

Cullen gave her a sympathetic smile. "It's not too bad here. I had a harder time when I was in Chicago. That was really far from home."

"You lived in Chicago?" Marcus paused, holding the glass he had raised to drink.

Cullen nodded. "I went to law school there."

"University of Chicago?"

"Yes, sir."

"Impressive program." Marcus directed his gaze to Nye as if to see if she realized the worth of the credentials.

Cullen felt the urge to tell Marcus his daughter couldn't care less, but he refrained and settled for saying, "I enjoyed it."

His gaze returned to Nye. Her stress was obvious in the lines on her brow and the fullness of the plate that held her barely touched food. He watched her take a bite. She chewed deliberately, as if the food were tasteless.

The sinking feeling that had grown in Cullen's stomach during the meal prevented him from enjoying it much either. He shouldn't have come.

After pushing himself to finish the onslaught of projects at the firm yesterday, Cullen had found himself with a rare lull in the density of his workload by the afternoon. The timing couldn't have been better when his grandfather called and unknowingly provided Cullen with the very excuse he needed to see Nye. If it hadn't been for Granddad's insistence that Cullen check on Nye because of her cold, he would have felt obligated to visit his grandfather instead. That's what Cullen should have been doing tonight, since he still had a respite from work overload, but Caroline had caught him at a weak moment.

Cullen had been eagerly planning his surprise visit to Nye's house when Caroline called to invite him to this anniversary dinner. The idea of spending two evenings in a row with Nye had sounded too wonderful to resist. He was going to mention the invitation to her when he saw her Friday night, but his mind was fully occupied with other things as soon as she had opened the door, looking so relaxed and utterly appealing.

Cullen never would have accepted Caroline's invitation if he had known his evening with Nye would end in disaster. As it was, he spent all morning deliberating over whether or not he should still go to the Sanders' house. He had picked up the phone, about to call with some pretext, but no excuse seemed plausible enough. Maybe the problem was that part of him still wanted to see Nye, hoping she would explain and help him to understand. What a fool he was to think coming would help.

That blue gaze flitted briefly to his face, but immediately moved away when she saw him watching her.

Frustration mingled with Cullen's remorse, as he felt the sting of rejection—another dismissal. He stabbed a broccoli floret and stuffed it in his mouth. He needed an excuse for his silence as his emotions teetered on the seesaw of the evening.

When Nye had peered past the pool table, looking for her father, Cullen's heart lurched. He didn't know whether to scowl or smile. He could hear her from the night before, telling him to go, and the pain of her words stung afresh like a cold knife pressing into a wound. But at the same time, the memory of the kiss they had shared was so vivid that he wanted to go to her and pull her into his arms. He hadn't known it was possible to feel so many contradictory emotions at once for the same person. Yet she seemed to feel nothing. Unless he could count the shock and displeasure he saw in her face when she realized he was there.

Even that was preferable to the way she refused to look at him now. Was he so wrong to expect an explanation? They had been having a wonderful time last night, then the dance, the kiss … and she threw him out. That deserved something. Anger overtook his hurt as Cullen glanced around the table, noting that he wasn't the only one finishing the meal in silence. The Sanders' anniversary dinner shouldn't be ruined because of what had happened between Cullen and Nye. Despite valiant attempts by Caroline and Marcus to make conversation, the celebration was feeling far from the festive.

He turned to Caroline. "I'm sure you must have told me, but how many years have you and Mr. Sanders been married?"

"Thirty years."

"Thirty beautiful years. The best of my life." Marcus gazed across the table at his wife, deep love glowing in his eyes.

"That's a long marriage for these days."

Marcus looked at Cullen as if he had forgotten others were at the table. "Yes, it is. We've been very blessed. I'll tell you, Cullen, it's so precious to find that one person God has picked out for you. If you find her, hold on tight because—"

Nye shoved her chair back and rushed from the room. Cullen thought he saw the glimmer of a tear on her cheek as she ran into the kitchen.

"Nye?" Oriana rose to follow.

"No. I'll go," Caroline said with a mother's practiced, brook-no-arguments tone.

Oriana reluctantly sank back into her chair as Caroline went to the kitchen. Oriana looked at her father, her face filled with sadness. "Oh, Daddy." She shook her head.

Marcus looked down, his shoulders sagging under an invisible burden.

Cullen wished someone would tell him what was going on—give him the reason for the pain that clung to this family.

But he didn't need an explanation to know how he felt about Nye. When she ran from the table, it took every bit of strength he had to keep himself from going after her. He had found that special woman God intended for him, and she was crying in the next room.

Her back to the doorway, Nye wiped away the one stray tear that escaped her control.

"Nye?"

Nye knew someone would follow, but she hadn't expected it to be her mother. Nye reached for the closest cabinet, hoping she remembered correctly that it held dessert plates. "I thought everyone might be ready for cheesecake." She nearly choked on her lame attempt at an excuse.

Her mother gently rested her hand on Nye's outstretched arm.

Nye slowly closed the door and pulled away, leaning against the counter behind her. She crossed her arms, avoiding her mother's gaze.

"Talk to me, sweetie."

"There's nothing to say." Nye raised her gaze, and her determination to be implacably composed almost faltered under her mother's soft expression of understanding. Nye remembered that look from when she was a little girl, when her mother was always ready to kiss Nye's scraped knee or explain away her growing pains. It meant comfort, security, peace.

"Honey, you're so unhappy. You need to let someone help you."

"I don't need help. I'm fine."

"No, you're not. Think about what you're doing. You won't even consider using your gifts, your God-given skills, to help Oriana's kids—"

"Don't start, Mother," Nye snapped.

Her mother raised her hands. "All right, I won't. But what about Cullen?"

Nye turned away, opened the cabinet, and yanked out the plates.

"Did you two have a fight?"

A plate clutched in her tense grip, Nye whirled to face her mother. "That's not your concern."

"All I know is you two were getting along beautifully, and now you won't even talk to him. The poor boy just sits there and watches you, and you refuse to look at him. Have you told him anything? About tango? About Dante?"

"Would you stop? Just stop!" Nye threw the plate to the floor where it smashed into pieces. She backed into the counter, touching her face with trembling fingers. She raised a shocked gaze to her mother.

"Nye, listen to me." Her voice was quiet and steady. "You're pushing Cullen away. Is that what you want?" She pursed her lips. "You lost Dante. Don't lose another man because you're too scared to love again."

What was he thinking? Cullen stared at the flames in the fireplace. They twisted, reached, ducked—like frustrated dancers searching for a rhythm.

After apologizing for the scene at dinner, Marcus had suggested Cullen go with him to the living room to wait for dessert. Cullen had been lost in thought since he sat on one of the black leather sofas. He was primarily occupied with trying to determine how he could have been so stupid as to have come this evening. He felt like the quintessential party crasher, ruining a celebration for the kind of marriage he could only dream of having. To make the situation worse, another wedge had been driven between him and Nye, separating them with more secrets and pain.

"Wishing you hadn't come?"

Cullen started and looked at Marcus, who watched him from an easy chair that angled toward the fireplace and the sofa where Cullen sat. Cullen had forgotten he wasn't alone. He hesitated, trying to formulate a safe response to the uncomfortably accurate question.

Marcus smiled slightly. "You don't have to answer that."

"No, it's all right. I … I'm afraid I might've ruined your celebration by being here. You can probably tell Nye and I had a … we aren't …" Cullen sighed and pushed a hand through his hair, not enjoying the rare loss for words. "To be honest, Mr. Sanders, I don't know what we are."

"It's Marcus, remember?"

Cullen nodded. "Marcus."

They sat in silence. Cullen stared into the fire, not wanting to attempt another explanation for something he couldn't possibly hope to understand.

"I don't usually think any man is good enough for my girls. But if you're the one God has picked for Nye, then you are good enough."

Cullen fought the urge to squirm, feeling a bit like a high school boy hoping to take Nye to the prom. "Thank you, sir."

"Don't thank me. I said 'if.'" He paused. "You still have a lot of work to do if you're going to win my daughter." His eyes narrowed. "Nye has had a lot of pain in her life. I don't want her to go through anymore."

"Yes, sir. I know she's been through something, but I can't get her to talk about it."

"Then I won't either. It's her story to tell when she's ready. I will say this, I would lay down my life to keep my girl from being hurt again." Firelight reflected in Marcus's dark eyes.

Cullen nodded.

"You may think I'm prying beyond my rights, but no one's going to toy with Nye while I'm around. Do you love my daughter?"

"Yes." The quickness of his own response took Cullen by surprise. He had never admitted it, never fully realized it before, yet his answer to the question was as natural as breathing. Of course he loved her. He didn't know when he had crossed the threshold between infatuation and love, but he suspected it had been much longer ago than he had realized.

"Then don't give up." Marcus's gaze softened with approval. "I've been praying God would break down the walls of that prison Nye's built. She hasn't healed, and I sometimes worry she never …" His eyes filled with moisture. He looked away and cleared his throat.

Cullen felt the stirrings of renewed determination. "I won't give up."

Marcus nodded. "I'll give you what help I can, but I'm afraid most of it's going to be up to you and the Lord."

Cullen's pulse surged with excitement. The realization of his feelings for Nye was intoxicating. In one moment, his mood changed from depressed to hopeful. He felt brave, confident, and happy. He couldn't stop the smile that crept onto his face. "In that case, I'll need more energy. How about some cheesecake?"

Marcus chuckled. "You know, I think you might be just what this family needs."

"Ow." Nye dropped the broken piece of a plate, surprised by a surge of sharp pain. Blood seeped from a cut in her palm. Great. Just what she needed. Her mother had told Nye not to pick up the pieces while she went for a broom, but Nye hadn't thought earthenware would be that sharp. Apparently, mother still knew best … sometimes.

Nye went to the sink and turned on the faucet. She moved her hand into the stream of water, wincing as the liquid flowed over the open wound. She turned off the water and looked around for a clean cloth. She opened a drawer next to her, hoping to find dishcloths instead of the silverware it contained.

A clean dishcloth appeared in front of her, held by a large hand that she knew well.

Cullen.

She reluctantly took the proffered cloth and dabbed her wet hand. "Thank you." She gently cleared her suddenly dry throat. She felt his closeness, his warmth, but she still couldn't face him.

"Seems like we're always meeting at the scene of an accident." He was closer than she thought. She could feel his breath on her neck as he spoke. "And you're always getting hurt."

She gathered her courage and turned to face him. She had to see what he meant by those words. No such luck. His eyes, now perilously close, held a glint of something she couldn't interpret.

"Let me see." He gently took her hand, cradling it in his as he had that morning on the highway. He ran his thumb lightly around the cut, making slow circles of sensation that made her forget any pain she had been feeling.

Her mind warring with her other desires, she pulled her hand from his. She turned away, her back to him, and placed the dishcloth on the counter. Her breathing uneven, she cleared her throat again. "I wanted to apologize ... last night ..."

"Nye, look at me."

She froze.

"Please."

She couldn't possibly stand her ground when he spoke with such tenderness. She took a step along the counter to get more space between them and turned.

She almost gasped at what she saw in his eyes this time. Dare she name it? Yes. It was love. Her first instinct was to melt into his arms. Then she realized the only thing she could do. She had to flee.

He must have seen her panic, because he stepped in front of her, blocking her path. He looked down at her, his face so very near.

She pressed against the counter, wildly hoping she could manage to think straight if she kept some small space between them.

"Do you want me to leave, Nye?" His deep voice was thick with emotion. "Is that what you want?" He slowly leaned closer and braced his arm against the cabinet behind her, boxing her in even more.

She had to look into his eyes.

They smoldered with barely bridled emotion.

"I don't think you really want me to go, but I will if it will make you happy." He lowered his head and stopped, inches from her face. "Say the word, and I'll get out of your life."

She couldn't think, couldn't breathe. He really meant it. He would leave. Isn't that what she wanted? She didn't want love, couldn't go through it again. *You're pushing him away.* Her mother's words echoed in her mind. Mother was right. If Nye lost Cullen, it would be no one's fault but her own. And she realized with frightening clarity that she didn't want to lose him at all.

"Is that what you want?" he whispered.

She licked her lips. "No," she breathed.

A smile slowly angled his mouth as he lowered it to meet hers.

She twined her arms around his neck as he pulled her to him and held her close. She felt as if every fiber of her being were coming alive, awakened from a deep sleep.

This would work. She had handled losing her second job so easily. It hadn't caused her any pain, any remorse. She was stronger now, strong enough to risk a relationship.

Cullen reluctantly ended the kiss, breathing raggedly as he pressed his forehead to hers.

Cradled in his arms, she relaxed, savoring his comforting warmth.

"Let me in, Nye. I need to know—"

She looked away. The anxiety tried to creep back, but she mentally pushed it away. She wouldn't let anything ruin this moment, destroy what she had found. She couldn't relive the past and still have the courage for a relationship with Cullen. Staring at the shattered remains of the plate on the floor, she whispered, "I can't. Please don't ask me."

He was silent for a moment. "Okay." When she didn't look up, he tightened his arms around her slightly. "Nye?"

She raised her gaze and saw understanding in his eyes.

"No more questions about the past. You tell me what you want, when you want. Just don't shut me out."

She nodded, biting her lip against tears of relief. She rested her head on his chest. In her mind, she heaved the door shut against the haunting memories of her past. This time, there would be no pain.

Chapter Fifteen

"Then David danced before the Lord with all his might."
–2 Samuel 6:14

Nye couldn't believe it when she neared the porch and spotted Russell sitting outside on the wooden bench. She smiled as she walked up the steps. "What are you doing out in the cold?"

"Afternoon to you, too." A responding smile brought a sparkle to Russell's eyes.

She laughed. "Hi. But you didn't answer the question."

"I'm waiting."

Deciding she could bear the icy air a little longer, she sat down beside him. "Waiting?"

"Yep." He turned back to the view of the shimmering white snow.

She had to admit, it was a lovely scene.

"What brought the sunshine to your face?"

She smiled again. She should have known it wouldn't take long for him to notice a change. "Your grandson." A sudden feeling of shyness came over her as she spoke the words. She slowly braved a look at Russell.

He watched her with gentle happiness glowing in his gaze. "Glad to hear it. What's he done?"

She took a breath. "We're going to start dating. But we're taking it slow."

He nodded. "No need to rush into anything. Just remember I don't have forever to see the wedding."

She threw him a shocked glance and caught the twinkle in his eyes. "Russell!" Though slightly exasperated, she was filled with affection for this elderly man. The connection they had shared from the first time they met had only grown stronger with the knowledge that he was Cullen's grandfather. Even so, the almost familial closeness she shared with him didn't ease her embarrassment from the topic of his teasing.

Surprising herself with the gesture, she looped her arm around his and made an effort to change the topic. "Speaking of taking things slowly, have you decided what to do about that offer?"

A sober expression came over his face. "It's in the kitchen … with my signature on it."

She looked for signs of regret or sadness and saw only calm resolve. "What made you change your mind?"

He was silent, looking at his land. "I want to show you something," he said at last.

That wasn't the answer she had expected. "Okay." She pulled her arm away and stood, as he reached for his crutches. She started toward the front door.

"Not in there. This way." He swung a crutch to point in the direction of the barn she had seen him come from that first day. With growing curiosity, she followed him off the side of the porch and down the path to the barn.

She shivered and wrapped her arms around herself as they walked, glad she had worn gloves. She glanced at Russell, wondering at his pensive expression. Respecting his silence, she kept her questions to herself as they reached the door.

He took out a key to unlock the latch.

She didn't think he even locked his house—why would he lock an old barn?

He pushed open the door, and she followed him inside, surprised by the warmth of the dark interior. Before her eyes could adjust to the dimness, he flicked a switch and lamps lit the large, open room, displaying an expansive collection of the finest wooden furnishings Nye had ever seen.

She walked among the tables, chairs, benches—staring in astonishment at the pieces that were all ornately carved with a skilled hand. She pulled off her glove and ran her fingers gently along the smooth wood of a mahogany dresser. These furnishings didn't just reflect good craftsmanship, they were art.

Past the furniture, she spotted tools on a work bench against a wall. Stunned, she turned to Russell. "Did you make these?"

He nodded.

She gazed at the exquisite collection. Though she no longer considered herself an artist, the creative expression before her touched her deeply, stirring latent emotions. "They're beautiful." She cleared her throat. "You're an artist."

He shook his head. "I don't know about that. Whatever I was, it's in the past now."

She looked at him, wondering why.

His crutches wedged under his arms, he raised his arthritic hands. "The Lord decided I had done enough carving years ago."

Nye stared at his shaking, stiffened fingers. She swallowed, the pain of his loss like salt in her own wound. "I'm so sorry."

"He has His reasons."

She looked away to hide her irritation with his meek attitude.

"But I don't always remember that."

Surprised by the comment, Nye met his gaze.

"I wanted you to see this. I needed to explain … to apologize."

"I don't understand."

"This …" he swept his arm to encompass the furniture, "is why I wouldn't sell."

Still confused, she waited for him to elaborate.

"Oh, I meant what I said about the casinos, but the other one … the shopping mall ... You were right. It didn't make sense for me to be against it." He sighed, looking at his handiwork. "It took me a while to figure it out myself. To figure out why I wouldn't take the offer—why I felt like I couldn't."

"I know you must have many memories here, Russell. There's nothing wrong with not wanting to let them go."

He shook his head. "It's not the memories. I can take those with me anywhere, but this … my art, you'd call it—that won't fit in an apartment or a little house in the city."

A lump lodged in her throat at the sight of the moisture that sprang to his eyes. "But you signed the contract."

"Funny how a man can get to thinking he's at peace with God's will, content to let go when the Lord takes away and just be thankful. Then all the sudden you see you've been holding something back."

"There must be a way to save this. You could look at storage options, or—"

"No. I've given it all away to that new homeless shelter downtown. It's a good, Christian shelter, and they need a lot of furniture. I was waiting for the truck that's going to haul it away when you got here."

She couldn't believe the contentment reflected in his eyes as he spoke. "You can't."

"Not without the Lord, but I talked to Him about it. I'm ready to let go. He's made it clear—it's time."

Bitterness welled in Nye's throat, bursting through the sympathy that had lodged there. "So just like that, you have to be happy about it? You just give up?" She hated herself for speaking so harshly to Russell, but she couldn't hold back her anger at the God who would do such a thing to a faithful, gentle old man.

Russell watched her closely with his unnervingly perceptive gaze. "You've lost something precious."

How did he see so much? She looked away, hoping to hide whatever remaining secrets he may not have discovered.

"It's in your eyes," he said, answering her unspoken question. "I saw it that first day you were standing there, shivering on my porch." He paused, as if making a decision. "Have I shown you the other picture I keep with me?" He reached into his pocket and pulled out another wallet-sized photo. He extended it toward her.

She moved closer to look. It was the image of a young man dressed in an army uniform. The aged photograph, clutched in Russell's arthritic fingers, trembled with the vibrations of his hand. "Gary. My son." His voice caught.

For a moment, Nye's bitterness softened as he wiped away a tear that coursed down his cheek.

"He was killed in Vietnam. We had nineteen years with him."

Renewed fury mixed with the grief Nye felt for Russell.

How could he still cling to the idea of a loving God? Such blindness made her sick.

He placed the small photo of his wife with the one of Gary and carefully slid the pictures into his pocket. "You know why I keep these with me?"

Not trusting herself to speak, she shook her head.

"I want to remember."

Remember? The pain of Dante's death clung to Nye, overshadowing every moment she breathed. She didn't need to carry reminders. She couldn't begin to comprehend why Russell would want to be reminded of his losses, and she couldn't fathom how he could possibly forget.

There was a honk in the driveway, and Nye waited as Russell went to meet the men who came to cart away his furniture. She swallowed past the sour taste in her mouth when they entered the barn like executioners there to select prisoners for the gallows.

Russell helped them load a stunning armoire that should have been in an art gallery or sold with the rest of the collection for a small fortune. The pieces probably wouldn't garner enough money to allow Russell to keep his ranch, but he could at least be more comfortable and secure as he aged. Nye knew what his response would be to that idea.

He didn't want money, he would say, he only cared about serving God—a God who repaid such devotion by stripping Russell of everything he held dear.

Resentment threatening to choke her, Nye turned away and left the barn. She couldn't bear to see any more. She shouldn't have let herself become so attached to Russell. That was the only reason his needless loss bothered her so greatly.

As she sank into the driver's seat of her car and started the engine, she glanced at the clock. She only had an hour to get ready for her first real date with Cullen, but she was hardly in the right frame of mind to enjoy it.

She took a deep breath and released it, trying to let go of her tension. Determined to recapture the cheerful optimism she had felt when she drove up the driveway, Nye threw the car into reverse and pushed all thoughts of Russell from her mind. She would not let anything destroy the happiness she had only just tasted.

Chapter Sixteen

*"And those who were seen dancing were thought to be insane
by those who could not hear the music."*
– Friedrich Nietzsche

Cullen watched the actors on stage. The play had garnered positive reviews, and he had wanted to see this production for some time, but now he was so distracted that he was missing about ninety percent of the drama. He couldn't believe Nye, this beautiful, fascinating woman, was sitting beside him. He checked out of the corner of his eye every few minutes, just to see if she was really there. When he looked again, she caught him.

A little thrill shot through his veins at the cautious happiness that gleamed in her eyes as she smiled, brightening the darkness of the theater. She seemed so relaxed tonight, so at ease. He had never seen her look more breathtaking. The change in her was almost enough to make him forget the nagging doubts that had been hounding him all day.

She turned back to watch the play, and Cullen pretended to do the same. She wanted a relationship with him. She had decided to date him. Why couldn't that be enough? Yet Cullen couldn't shake the feeling that he should not have agreed to ignore her past, to accept not knowing what caused the sadness that had kept her from him.

When he had entered the kitchen at her parents' house that night, Cullen intended to confront Nye about her feelings for him, as well as whatever she was hiding. When she admitted that she wanted him in her life, he felt as if he had been handed something infinitely precious. But as soon as he broached the subject of her past, she started pulling back. The fear of losing what he had in his grasp for only a moment overwhelmed his better judgment and he gave in. He had avoided the possibility of losing Nye, but what was he willing to sacrifice for that reason?

It didn't help that Grant had seemed to echo Cullen's every doubt when Cullen called his friend from his apartment to give an update on the events with Nye.

"But if she doesn't tell you, do you think your relationship will ever become what you want?" Grant's question had hung over the line as Cullen tried to think of a response. "I mean, it just seems like it might not get very far."

Cullen blinked, silent.

Grant sighed. "That came out wrong. I'm just wondering if you can really know her or help her if she doesn't trust you enough to tell you what happened. You know what I mean?"

"Yeah, I know. I just ... if I push her, she'll run away again. I won't have any chance at all." Cullen shoved his hand through his hair.

"Something else has been bothering me. You're not gonna like it."

Cullen swallowed. "Go ahead."

"Do you know where Nye stands spiritually?"

Cullen sagged onto the barstool, feeling like he'd been struck. "She's a Christian." He didn't like the defensive note in his voice or the anxiety that curdled in his stomach.

"Are you sure?" Grant had pressed. "You know she doesn't go to church regularly. Have you actually talked to her about God? What she believes?"

Vibration in Cullen's suit jacket pocket startled him out of the memory. It was the second time his phone had alerted him to a new message since the play had started. Cullen knew it was risky to schedule a date and be out of the office on a weeknight, but he wasn't about to forego an evening with Nye just to bolster his reputation at work. He hadn't expected anyone from the office would try to get hold of him tonight.

Wondering what the urgency was all about, he quietly sneaked out his phone and checked the messages, careful to expose the lit screen for only a brief moment.

Blanchard. Terrific. Not only had the partner noticed Cullen was absent from the office, but he also needed Cullen to draft a disclosure schedule for a purchase agreement by morning. How was he supposed to do that? He planned to take Nye to a restaurant after the play. He stifled a sigh. He was looking forward to the time with Nye, but the evening now promised to be longer than he anticipated if he had to go into work after dinner.

The actors walked off the stage and applause broke out around Cullen. Disappointed that his distractions had caused him to miss the end of the play, he half-heartedly joined in applauding the actors as they returned for the curtain call.

Nye leaned close, sending a warm surge of awareness through Cullen.

"Is everything okay?" she asked. "I saw you check your phone."

"Just work. Nothing major."

"Are you sure?"

"Yeah." He gave her a reassuring smile, though he felt tension slowly building in his shoulders. He fought against it, trying to relax. He would get the work done one way or another.

They started out of the aisle, moving with the rest of the audience members toward the exit. With Nye pressed close to him because of the crowd, Cullen forgot his stress as his senses went into overdrive.

When they reached the lobby, she looked up at him. "Where are we going for dinner? Let me guess—someplace Italian?" The corner of her mouth rose in a curvy, teasing smile he'd never seen before.

The effect was breathtaking. He had to gather his scattered thoughts before he could formulate a response. "Of course." He grinned, lost under the spell of the charming new sparkle in her eyes. "Sometimes I think God must've made Italian food just for me."

Cullen tried not to notice the way she looked away at his words. She was probably just distracted by those people who walked past. It didn't have to be a reaction to the mention of God.

She turned back to him. "Why so grim?"

He mustered a smile. "Just thinking." Now he couldn't even be open and honest with her. "You want to wait here? I'll get our coats."

"Oh, okay. Thanks."

As he worked his way through the crowd to the coat check station, Cullen battled the relentless urging that he needed to ask about her faith. He was almost positive she was a Christian. He had assumed as much from the day he met her family at church, and Nye was helping with the church's anniversary celebration. But even if he was right, he was coming to suspect that her relationship with God was far from healthy.

He had probably recognized the signs earlier, but his feelings for her had caused him to turn a blind eye to more than one problem. He shouldn't date a woman who wasn't a Christian, and he knew it. But wasn't it okay to be involved with a Christian who was only struggling?

Cullen retrieved their coats from the attendant and headed back to Nye. A new kind of tension tightened his muscles as he approached her and tried to think of a way to broach the question of her relationship with God.

He held her coat open and took a deep breath as she slipped her arms into the sleeves. "Nye?"

"Yes?" She stepped away and turned to him, belting her coat.

His throat tightened. "There's something I wanted to ask you." He saw a flash of panic in her eyes and rushed to reassure her. "Not about the past. I promised."

She nodded and watched him guardedly.

"It's something else. I …" He glanced at the people who passed them as they headed for the exit. Starting to feel like a coward, he forced himself to meet her gaze.

Her expression grew increasingly wary as she waited.

Cullen couldn't remember when he'd ever felt so nervous. He licked his lips. "Are you …" How could he even ask this? "How do you feel about Go—"

The vibrating of his phone was like a shock to his taut nerves.

"About what?" She watched as he took out the electronic device. "What is it?"

He wouldn't normally read his messages while talking to Nye, but at this moment, he welcomed the interruption. "I'm sorry. Do you mind if I check this?"

"Of course not."

His stress level surged to new heights as he read the message.

"Bad news?" She watched him with a concerned expression.

"It's from Blanchard."

"The partner you were talking about?"

He nodded, glad he had told her enough about Blanchard for her to understand the situation. "Now he's strongly suggesting I get to the office as soon as possible. He wants a disclosure schedule within the next hour. His last message said tomorrow morning." Cullen clenched his jaw in frustration.

"Do you need to go?"

"And skip dinner? Of course not." Though he meant the words, he felt like he was being yanked in two directions and stretched to his limits.

The feeling must have shown on his face, because Nye's brow furrowed. "Cullen, you should go. I don't mind, really. If you don't go, this partner is only going to make it harder for you. We'll get dinner another time."

He searched her blue eyes. They held only genuine concern and understanding. He swallowed, feeling terrible that he had somehow ended up in this situation. "You're sure? You really don't mind?"

She shook her head. "I really don't."

He sighed. "Okay, but I'm still taking you home."

She shrugged. "It's out of the way. Why don't I just take a taxi?"

"What kind of a date do you think this is? You're getting a full escort home." He tried to hide his mortification under a layer of humor.

She rewarded his effort with a smile. "Yes, sir."

His heart lurched in response to the mischievous glint in her eyes. Though he hated the thought of cutting their time short for work, he was glad Blanchard's message had stopped him from asking about her faith and making what could have been a fatal mistake. There was no way he would risk pushing this woman away. He would bide his time and wait until she learned to trust him with even her deepest pain. He only hoped that decision wouldn't blow up in his face.

Nye had to smile at the sweet way Cullen kept apologizing as they walked on the sidewalk in front of the Wilson Performing Arts Center, heading for the parking lot.

"I'm so sorry about this," he said again.

"Cullen, it's fine. I mean it. I used to have a demanding job, too, remember? I know what it's like."

He smiled, but the expression looked strained. "That's right, you did. I forgot to ask, have you found any leads for a job yet?"

She tilted up her coat collar, hoping to block the biting

wind. "The pickings are very slim in Harper right now. There are a few possibilities in Metcalf."

He glanced at her. "Metcalf? That's over two hours away. You wouldn't move, would you?"

She hesitated, not sure how to answer. She could tell by his cautious and surprised tone this was a delicate subject. It was for her, too. She wouldn't have chosen to move right now, especially because she was just starting a relationship with Cullen, but she needed a job.

She opted for a completely honest response. "I really don't want to, but at this point …" She trailed off as they passed promotional posters fixed to the wall of the building, and she caught the image of a dancer. She immediately turned away, but not before Cullen had noticed the direction of her gaze.

"Looks like there was a dance performance in the other theater tonight. I wondered why there were so many people leaving. It didn't seem like they all could've been at the play."

Nye felt him watching her as he spoke, but she couldn't look at him. She wasn't going to tell him anything about her past, if that's what he was waiting for.

He stopped walking and turned to her.

She held her breath, sure he was going to demand an explanation.

He reached for her hand and gently grasped it in his. "I'm not going to press you."

She released the breath.

"Will you try to trust me?"

She lifted her head and searched his eyes in the light cast from a nearby street lamp. How could she not trust the gentleness reflected in those dark brown depths? She nodded.

He smiled. "Your hand is freezing. Let's get you to the car." Before she could pull away, he linked her arm through his and led her toward the parking lot, covering her cold fingers with his warm hand.

She relaxed as they walked. She savored an inward thrill at the feel of Cullen's strength and warmth permeating his coat. It was hard to believe it had only been a few days since she had decided to pursue a relationship with him. During that brief time, she had felt as though she were a completely new person, living in a transformed world. Everything around her seemed more beautiful and alive. Even on this frigid night, the snow looked whiter and the stars gleamed more brilliantly than ever because Cullen was at her side. Why had she fought her attraction to him for so long? She could barely remember.

It didn't matter anymore, for at this moment she felt like she could tackle anything. She was finally shaking free of her past, and she knew now that she had the inner strength to handle the future—a future that was looking brighter by the moment.

The acrid smell of cigarette smoke reached her nostrils as she and Cullen passed the corner of the Wilson Center and turned to cross the parking lot.

A dark figure, clothed in black, slumped against the wall.

Nye might not have seen him at all if not for the orange glow of the cigarette he held between his fingers. Dim light from the parking lot lamps fell across his shiny black hair and angular features, casting random shadows over his unseasonably tanned skin. There was something strangely familiar about his muscular stature and the way he braced one foot against the wall behind him.

He turned his head in Nye's direction.

She looked away. Memories surged from the back of her mind where she thought she had safely hidden them. She willed herself to relax. It wasn't him. It could not be him.

She instinctively pressed closer to Cullen as they headed for the car, and the resulting hyperactivity of her senses banished the fears that briefly threatened her newfound happiness.

He glanced down at her with surprise.

She blushed and looked away. On the other hand, maybe a little apprehension was the safer experience.

"*Pajarita?*"

She jerked to a halt at the sound of the familiar voice behind her and the name only one person had ever called her. She slowly turned. No ... Please, no.

"Nicanor ..." She mouthed the name, but no sound emerged. Her legs went numb. She started to sink. She vaguely registered some pressure on her arms, then under her legs, her

back, but she was still drowning, drowning. She saw Dante—
laughing, teasing, happy. He smiled at her, that special smile.
Then he lay in a cold coffin, pale, lifeless.

"Nye?" A voice cut through the chilling memory. "Nye,
can you hear me?"

She slowly opened her eyes. She was on the ground, but
lying in Cullen's arms, cradled against his firm chest. His face
was hidden in shadows under the bright lamp that blinded her.
She couldn't see his eyes, couldn't see anything but that garish
light. She started to push away, but he tightened his hold.

"Rest, *pajarita*," said a different voice, tinged with a
Spanish accent. "You shouldn't stand on your own yet." The
man moved into her line of sight, blocking the glaring lamp.

Nye focused on the dark, chiseled features of the face she
had never expected to see again.

Nicanor. Everything came back in a rush as her strength
returned. "Let me go." Her tone, like cold steel, was apparently
enough to jar Cullen. He gave her a surprised look as he
quickly, but gently, helped her stand. Desperately seeking an
escape, she spun away.

Cullen grasped her wrist. "Nye, wait. Please."

She jerked out of his hold. "No." It was all she could say
as she gave in to her urge to flee and ran down the sidewalk.
The icy ache clenched her heart. The swirling memories, the
pain—it all came back. She wrapped her arms around herself

and slowed her pace. As she trudged ahead, she couldn't see anything but Dante's face. Not smiling, not laughing. Just dead.

Chapter Seventeen

"To what is all driving? What is the morning you speak of? ...
The beginning of the Great Game, of the Great Dance ..."
–C. S. Lewis

"Thank you, Lord," Cullen murmured, when the door to Nye's house opened. But it was Oriana, and not Nye, who stood inside.

"Cullen. Thank the Lord," Oriana echoed Cullen's sentiment as she motioned him in.

"I tried to call, but there was no answer."

She nodded. "I was at the movies with some friends from church. Just got home." The usual happy gleam in her eyes was tarnished with worry. "Nye's in her room and won't open the door. She won't tell me anything. Won't even let Jordan in."

The dog lay along the back of the couch, head resting on his paws and looking as forlorn as Cullen felt.

"What happened?"

Cullen raked his hand through his hair, ready to burst with frustration. "I wish I knew. There was a man in the parking lot at the Wilson after the play. He said something to Nye and ... it was like the life just left her. She collapsed, passed out ..."

Oriana's eyes widened.

"Just a couple seconds," he added, trying to reassure her. "When she came to, she saw the guy again and took off."

"Do you know who he was? Did he say?"

Cullen shook his head. "He wouldn't give me his name. Didn't even answer my questions. He just kept muttering that he had to talk to Nye. He asked me where she lived—I wasn't about to tell him."

"What did he look like?"

"Close to my height, maybe a little shorter—dark hair, dark coloring. He had an accent and said something to Nye in Spanish, I think." Cullen squinted, trying to remember anything else that would help. "She mouthed something before she fell, maybe his name."

"What was it?"

"I don't know," he snapped. He grimaced and fought to calm himself. "I'm sorry, I … I just feel so helpless."

She looked at him with compassion in her gaze. "It's okay."

His mouth twisted into a humorless smile. "I'm afraid it might not be. I—Wait." The image of Nye's face before she collapsed cleared in his mind. "'N.' His name started with an 'n.' Something like Nick or—"

"Nicanor." Oriana's face paled.

"Yes. That's it." Cullen brightened, as if the discovery somehow brought a ray of hope.

"Then he was looking for her," Oriana said, as if to herself.

"Who is he?"

"He's the man who killed her fiancé."

Cullen felt like his heart dropped to his shoes.

Oriana inhaled a deep breath. "Well, that's how Nye sees it anyway. I've never met him." She paused when she noticed Cullen's stunned expression. "Oh, my. She didn't tell you?"

"Tell me what? That she was engaged? That her fiancé died?" He clenched his fists and looked away, staring sightlessly at the tan floor tiles in the entry. "No. She didn't tell me anything."

"I thought … you two were so happy after Saturday, and she told me you were going to date. I just assumed …"

"Will you tell me? Please. I have to know why Nye keeps putting up this wall between us."

Oriana's gaze softened as she studied him. "You really love her, don't you?"

He could only nod, not trusting himself to speak past the tightness in his throat.

"Let's sit down."

He silently followed her into the living room and sat on the couch while she took the nearby armchair. He tried to brace himself for whatever she was about to tell him.

"Dante Reese, Nye's fiancé, drowned three years ago." Oriana's eyes pooled with deep sadness.

"There's more, isn't there?"

She nodded and crossed her arms as if trying to warm herself. "He was also her tango partner."

Cullen stared at Oriana, beginning to put the pieces together.

"Unless you're a dancer or you knew her then, it's hard to really comprehend what that means." Oriana sighed and stared into the unlit fireplace. "Nye met Dante in New York the year after she graduated. He was a couple years older than her and was already making a name for himself as a dancer. I think Nye might've been a bit star struck when she first saw him, but the feeling was mutual, and they fell in love." Oriana glanced at Cullen as if checking to see if this was too difficult for him to hear.

It was. He prayed for strength as he tried to swallow the bitter taste that instinctively rose to his mouth at the idea of Nye loving another man. *Lord, forgive me.*

"They started to dance as partners and became a sensation," Oriana continued. "They were hailed as the bright future of tango. I saw them dance together a few times." She looked at Cullen with an awed expression. "It ... they were beautiful. They danced as if they were one person. I've never seen anything like it. They were so connected." She paused. "Maybe too much."

One person. Nye with someone else. Cullen tried to balance the words with what he felt for her.

Oriana smiled sadly, as moisture glistened in her eyes. "But I don't think I've ever seen her as happy as she was then. She was doing what she loved with the man she loved. Their oneness wasn't just on the dance floor. They did everything together, always inseparable." Her smile faded. "Then Dante ..." She wiped away a tear that coursed down her cheek. "I'm fuzzy on the details. Nye barely talked about it, even then."

Oriana glanced at Cullen. "I guess Nicanor convinced Dante to go out on his sailboat. They often went sailing when they had time. Nye usually went, too. No long trips, just fooling around off the coast. I guess this time Nye said they shouldn't go because they needed to rehearse. They were going on tour." She paused, biting her lip. "The tour was also going to be their honeymoon."

The knife turned in Cullen's heart with those words, even as it began to ache for Nye and the gravity of her pain.

"Dante and Nye fought about it, and Dante went with Nicanor. They got caught out in a bad storm. Nye had always said Nicanor was irresponsible with the boat. Took risks, skipped the lifejackets, didn't check the weather. Nicanor came back and Dante ... didn't. He died exactly one week before their wedding day." Oriana sniffed and tried to wipe the wet tracks off her face. "I guess you know the rest."

Cullen nodded, speechless. His jealousy faded as compassion for Nye took over, making him feel as if the suffering she had experienced was his own.

"Dante was a wonderful Christian man. He shared Nye's passion for dance and seemed to bring her closer to the Lord." Oriana shook her head. "She was so attached to him, so … I don't know … he was everything to her. It's like he became her whole life. When she lost him, she lost her reason to live. It nearly destroyed her."

Cullen took a breath and hesitated, afraid to ask the question that had been burning a hole in his conscience. "Does Nye know the Lord?"

Understanding reflected in Oriana's eyes as she met his gaze. "Yes, I believe she does. We accepted Christ on the same night when we were children. I'm sure she was sincere, but when Dante died, her faith shattered. She blamed Nicanor, Dante, herself—God most of all. She's done her best to push Him away, but I don't think He'll let her go so easily." She gave Cullen an encouraging smile. "I suspect that may be why He sent you."

Cullen tried to return the smile, wishing he could share her optimism. At least he finally knew. He could understand the sorrow in Nye's gaze, the fear of caring and losing that made her run away. He looked at the person who had extended this lifeline. "Thank you."

"You're welcome." She watched him for a moment. "What are you going to do now?"

He answered with the conviction rooted deep in his soul: "Pray."

Chapter Eighteen

"There seems no plan because it is all plan: there seems no centre because it is all centre."
–C. S. Lewis

They danced by the ocean. The dancer's smile was soft and gentle, his arms warm and strong as he held her close. The smile faded. She felt cold. He dropped his arms and turned away. He walked toward the waves that grew bigger with each step. Her limbs frozen and weak, she didn't try to follow. A boat appeared, carrying a tall, dark man. He stretched out a hand to the dancer. The dancer kept walking. He went deeper, deeper until a wave rushed over his head and swallowed him completely. She watched, helpless, waiting for the dark figure to do something. "Save him!" she called. The dark shadow just looked at her, then at the water. He rowed away. He was engulfed in darkness.

"Save him ... please ..." Nye murmured into her pillow, turning away from the hand that gently shook her shoulder.

"Nye, wake up." A soft, feminine voice came from somewhere above her. "Nye, sweetie, it's okay. Just wake up." Oriana's voice registered.

Nye opened her eyes. "What happened?"

"You were having a nightmare." Oriana sat on the edge of the bed.

Nye pushed herself up against the headboard and drew in a shaky breath, trying to calm her racing pulse. Her nightgown clung to her skin, clammy with sweat. She pushed her damp hair away from her face with trembling fingers.

Jordan whimpered softly from the floor by her bed.

Beginning to focus, Nye met her sister's concerned gaze. "It's certainly not the first time. Go back to bed, Oriana."

"I know you don't want me to come in your room when that happens, but I couldn't just lie there and listen to you like that. You sounded like you were in so much pain." Her voice cracked slightly, and she bit her lip.

Nye wished she could reach out and banish the sorrow in Oriana's eyes that seemed to have spread from Nye to her sister. But she couldn't muster the strength. She was dead inside. She tried to manage a few words. "I know. Thank you."

"Someone has to help you, Nye."

"No." Nye kept her voice firm. "This happened to me, no one else. I have to handle it by myself." She fixed Oriana with a glare. "And don't you dare start telling me how I need to find God again."

"What about Cullen?"

Nye barely hid the stab of pain the question inflicted. She turned away and stepped over Jordan to head for the bathroom.

"Why won't you talk to him?"

The fresh image of Cullen as she had pushed him away, something she thought she would never do again, clouded her vision. She closed her eyes against the pain, then opened them and made herself continue forward.

"I told him."

Nye halted.

"I told him everything."

Nye slowly turned. Her sister's steady gaze held none of the guilt Nye thought should be there. A spark of anger flared in her dead heart. "You had no right."

"No." Oriana pushed off the bed and stalked over to Nye with a rare show of temper. "You had no right not to tell him." Her gaze softened as she stood in front of Nye. "Do you have any idea how much he loves you?"

Nye looked away, swallowing the sob that threatened to escape. "He can't."

"He can't or you can't? Nye, just today you were so happy. You were letting yourself live again. Why are you giving all of that away?"

The haunting memories of Dante that swirled in her mind and the icy pressure on her heart formed Nye's answer. She couldn't put that kind of torment into words. She turned away once more and walked toward the bathroom.

Oriana sighed. "Okay. Goodnight then."

Nye reached in the bathroom to flick on the light.

"You can try all you want," Oriana's words carried from the door to Nye's room, "but you can't hide from them forever." Her voice filled with sadness as she continued. "Not Cullen, not Dante, and especially not God."

Nye turned just in time to see the door close behind her sister.

Nye stared at the clock as she sat on the side of her bed, feet touching the floor. The numbers on the clock changed slowly. *11:23 … 11:24 … 11:25.* It seemed to tick off the progress of the headache that began somewhere deep beneath her skull and spread outward, likely destined to explode into a migraine. She wasn't surprised by the reappearance of this demon that had plagued her in the days immediately following Dante's death. She expected such a follow-up to her restless night.

Jordan nudged her hand with his nose, whimpering. He always seemed to sense when she was in pain. Usually, he was able to distract or comfort her. Not today.

She rested her hand on his head and looked at the clock again. Despite staring at it all morning, she didn't know how many hours had passed since she gave up trying to sleep. She hadn't bothered to dress or get up. What was the point?

She looked at the window, wincing at the burst of pain in her head from the outdoor light. She hadn't pulled the shade last night, but sheets of driving snow blocked the view of anything beyond a few feet from the window. Even there, the only sight was a white wall of seemingly endless snow. Watching the blizzard-like conditions was like seeing inside her soul.

She raised a hand to rub her eyes. They were crusty and dry from her futile attempts to rest. She couldn't sleep, couldn't think without pain. She woke from nightmares only to collide with the ache of reality. Seeing Nicanor hadn't just revived old memories, it had completely resurrected the devastation of her loss. Dante suddenly became so present, and the memories became living realities so palpable that Nye felt the agony of his death as if it had just happened.

How could she possibly have dared to think she could love again and risk this result? She didn't even have one whole day of happiness with Cullen before Nicanor appeared to revive her pain. God just couldn't let her have that.

She swallowed the bile rising in her throat. If she let herself love Cullen, she was sure God wouldn't hesitate a moment to crush her by again ripping away what she held most dear. Three years ago, she had questioned why God picked her out for a seemingly systematic experiment in destruction of the human soul. But it was fruitless to seek answers from Someone who had forsaken her and tried to smash her spirit—the very things He had promised never to do. God was silent when she screamed for help and mute when her soul curled up to die.

There were no answers, no explanations when a person was just a pawn in a game. There was only survival. Love didn't fit into that kind of existence.

The image of Dante's lifeless face flashed before her. Anguish squeezed her heart until she was barely able to breathe. No taste of love was worth this.

The phone shrieked beside her bed. Nye jumped. She stared at the phone as it rang again … then again … and again. The answering machine clicked on. She barely listened as Oriana's cheerful recording filled the room. Nye hoped it wasn't Cullen again.

"Hello." An unfamiliar woman's voice came over the machine. "I'm calling from St. John's Hospital regarding Oriana Sanders—"

Nye snatched the receiver on the last word. "Hello?"

"Hi. Who am I speaking with?"

"Nye Sanders." Fear clutched her heart. "Oriana's sister."

"Can you come to the hospital, ma'am?"

"What happened?" Nye's voice trembled. She waited what seemed like an eternity for the words she'd give her life not to hear.

"Your sister's been in an accident."

Chapter Nineteen

"You have turned for me my mourning into dancing ..."
–Psalm 30:11

Nye focused on the bright blue of the nurse's scrubs as the woman led the way down a hall of the ICU. The fluorescent lights and sterile air in the cavernous corridor made Nye feel as frozen as when she had left her car and leaned into the blinding snow to reach the hospital. A two hour wait with her parents in the colorless waiting room had done nothing to warm the chill that ran through her veins.

The nurse stopped at an open door and turned to Nye. She gestured toward the room. "Just five minutes, okay?" She flashed a perfunctory smile and walked away.

Though Nye had let her parents have the first two short visits, she still wasn't ready to see her sister. She already had the picture of Dante permanently burned in her memory. She couldn't bear another. Not Oriana.

Nye took a deep breath, instantly regretting it when a piercing pain surged against her skull. She closed her eyes until the pressure of the migraine returned to the more tolerable sensation of her head being squeezed in a vise. Opening her eyes, she forced herself to step into the room. The whirring and beeping of machines greeted her as she slowly approached the bed.

A woman Nye barely recognized lay under blankets, tubes, and other medical paraphernalia she couldn't identify. The doctor had said Oriana was in a coma but was stable. She didn't look "stable." She was pale and lifeless, like a machine being kept alive by a million power cords.

A rush of hot fury fueled the pressure of Nye's migraine until she thought her head might explode. This wasn't Oriana. This wasn't the sparkling treasure of happiness that was her sister. Oriana had been stolen—ripped away like Nye's job, like tango, like Dante. The destruction of one life apparently wasn't enough. God had to take away her new career, Cullen, and now Oriana. When would it stop? Just when Nye thought she had reached rock bottom and had tasted more bitterness than a person could take, God had one final blow—enough to finish her once and for all.

Why Oriana? Why not just kill Nye, when she had spun out on the ice those weeks ago? The question had to be asked—even a child with his playthings would have to care for one as precious and beautiful as Oriana. He would want to protect her, to keep her safe.

Tears that wouldn't flow burned at the backs of Nye's eyes, as she looked at her sister's pale face. How could Oriana hold fast to a God who would do this to her, to their family?

Nye whirled and rushed from the room. As she dashed through the doorway, she crashed into something hard.

Cullen.

He gripped her arms and gently set her away from him. "Are you all right?"

She blinked. The impact of running into him amplified the surging in her head, but she welcomed the physical pain as a brief distraction from her emotional torture. "What …?" She cleared her dry throat. "What are you doing here?"

"Your mother called me. Nye … I'm so sorry."

The gentleness in his gaze was like a warm hand reaching to soften her heart, and she yearned to return to his arms. But there was no safety there—only the threat of more loss, greater agony. She looked away. "You shouldn't have come." She stared at the large letters attached to the wall: INTENSIVE … CA—

"Nye, you promised you wouldn't shut me out."

She looked at the tiles of the white floor. "You shouldn't have come."

"Maybe not." A firmness crept into his voice. "But I'm here."

She lifted her startled gaze to his face. She searched his eyes and flinched at the love and sympathy she saw there.

"Explain it to me, Cullen. Why Oriana?" She spit out the words with anger Cullen didn't deserve. "Why not me? I'm the one He hates."

"Nye—" Cullen reached for her.

"No." She jerked away. "She loves God. He shouldn't use her in some game to get at me."

"That's not what—"

She veered around Cullen and jogged toward the doors that led to the waiting area. She knew what he was going to say: that's not what God was doing. God loves Oriana. He loves you. It's God's will, He's in control. She had heard it all before. The circle of lies and clichés swirled in her memory. Christians who had never tasted suffering or had programmed themselves to accept everything like puppets on strings had driven Nye to the breaking point with their well-intentioned platitudes. She didn't need any more.

She shoved open the door and stalked toward her parents.

They sat in chairs along the wall, clutching each other's hands. Her mother used a soaked tissue to dab ineffectually at the tears cascading down her mascara-streaked cheeks. "Why did she go out?" Her mother's voice trembled as Nye slowed her approach, unnoticed by her parents. "I told her the snow was going to get worse. They had canceled school—"

"Shhh." Nye's father pulled her mother into an embrace. "You said she wanted to pick up a boy's backpack for him, right? He had left it at school?"

Nye's mother nodded against his chest.

"Honey, you know how important those kids are to

Oriana. She'd do anything for them, and she wouldn't regret it."

Her mother's body shook with a sob.

Her father looked up at Nye. Her heart almost broke at the raw anguish in his eyes. She had thought going through this herself was torture. She never anticipated what it might be like to watch her parents suffer. Did God have no mercy at all? The sobs that racked her mother's body and the helpless gasp of her father as he started to cry gave her the answer.

Cullen wandered down the darkened hallway of the hospital, desperately wishing he knew what to do. He looked at his watch. It was late—nine thirteen. He should probably go home. But he couldn't leave now any more than he could when Nye had brushed past him outside Oriana's room.

Nye probably thought he had left, but he had instead followed the winding, seemingly endless halls, not knowing where to go. He wasn't welcome to stay but going to his apartment or work would be pointless. Remembering the torment in Nye's eyes would make him unable to sleep or concentrate on anything else. At least if he stayed in the same building, he felt close to her, within reach if she should turn to him.

If not for the ache of his heart, he would have smiled at the resilience of his hopefulness where Nye was concerned. It never seemed to die, no matter how many times she rejected him. For that brief moment in the ICU, he thought she might finally be ready to lean on him. When she asked him to explain why this was happening, she was asking him for help with her anguish. But how could he help when she wouldn't even listen? It was like she was more afraid of getting an answer for the pain than she was of the pain itself.

Who was he kidding anyway? He didn't have any answers. Even if she had given him a chance to respond, he had no idea what to say. He couldn't understand any of this either. He was helpless, and he despised the feeling.

He reached a doorway and read the sign on the wall beside it: CHAPEL. He stepped inside the dimly lit room. A sense of peace filled him as he walked to the front of the small chapel, passing a few empty rows of chairs. At the front of the room, a statue of Jesus, nailed to the cross, stood on an altar.

Cullen sagged into a chair near the front, his own weakness and helplessness washing over him like an ocean-powered wave. How could he have been so foolish as to think he was the one Nye needed, that he could save her from her agony?

He had been blessed with such a wonderful life—his family was healthy, he had a successful career, he even had an easy path to faith and spiritual growth. He could barely fathom the kind of pain Nye had endured in her lifetime. And now, to have tragedy hit her again, perhaps more excruciating than ever before. It seemed almost cruel. It was imbalanced, disproportionate—dare he think it? ... Unfair.

"Life isn't fair," his favorite Sunday school teacher had told him. If it were, she had explained more than once, no one would have their sins washed away and be offered eternal life when they had done nothing to earn such a gift.

That was all well and good when a person didn't encounter much suffering. But the argument didn't help Cullen understand why a lovely, vibrant young woman was lying in a coma or show him how to cope with watching the woman he loved suffer while he couldn't do a thing to help her.

He looked up, and his gaze rested on the statue of Jesus Christ. *Why, Lord?* He couldn't believe he was asking the question he had thought he was too spiritually mature to ever voice. God is in control, and we have to trust Him. That's what Cullen firmly believed, but that belief had never been so tested. *Lord, why are you letting Nye suffer again? Don't you see her agony? Don't you understand what this is doing to her?*

Tears blurred Cullen's vision. He wiped them away before they could fall and saw more clearly the statue—the nails in Christ's hands and feet, the anguish that twisted His face. Yes, God understood. He knew Nye's pain, her sorrow. He had suffered all of that and more. And because He had chosen to experience such torment, Nye, her parents, and Cullen didn't have to face their suffering alone. Cullen was sure Caroline and

Marcus knew that, but Nye seemed too blinded by the waves of oppression to see the hand that was reaching out to save her.

She wasn't the only one. Cullen had lost sight of God's promise that His people would have pain in this fallen world, but that He would always be with them in their suffering. Tears filled Cullen's eyes again as he saw himself. How had he come to take so many things for granted? His friends, his family, most especially his grandfather—anything could happen to them at any moment. Yet instead of savoring each opportunity to spend time with his loved ones, he had neglected those relationships. And for what? His job.

But the Lord had given Cullen his work, so didn't he have to do his best at it? Cullen immediately recognized the weakness of his instinctive excuse. He was certain God had guided him into law and given him the skills for the profession, but he also knew that he had neglected to involve God in every phase of his career.

It wasn't surprising that his priorities had become skewed. He focused so completely on performance, keeping his job, and obtaining a partnership that everything else, including his relationships with God and others, became secondary. How could he have gotten so confused? His purpose in life wasn't to succeed as a lawyer. It was to glorify God. Instead of working so hard to become a partner at the firm, he should have invested his energy into showing others what it meant to live for Christ, into cultivating relationships that would enable him to show God's love to others.

Forgive me, Father. As Cullen prayed the words, he felt the grace of God transforming his soul. With God's help, Cullen would never again take for granted what he had been given, including the chance to make a difference in the lives of people around him.

Cullen's phone vibrated. He pulled it out of his pocket, almost smiling at the test that came so soon after his resolution. He glanced at the screen. The message was from Blanchard.

With the peace of God's wisdom strengthening Cullen to his core, he stood and went to the hallway. Pausing beside a trashcan, he dropped the phone into it and walked away. He smiled at the satisfying thunk, feeling as though he was the one who had just taken hold of that hand and been pulled from the deep water to where he could breathe life once again. The feeling was worth the small hassle he'd have getting a new phone and number, one only his family and friends would have.

Cullen would call his grandfather as soon as he could get to a phone, but in the meantime, he would continue to pray. Not as he had prayed before, when he asked God to let him help Nye, to show her that she was safe in Cullen's love and could trust him despite her past. He wasn't Nye's redeemer— God was. And now more than ever, only God could save Nye from the despair of suffering without Him.

The monotonous beeping of the monitor that measured the strength of Oriana's life kept time with the pounding inside Nye's head. Her vision starting to blur from the migraine, Nye peered at her father from under the hand she braced against her forehead.

He sagged in a stiff chair near Oriana's bed, his head slumped to catch an elusive moment of sleep. Nye was glad he was able to escape from this horror, if only briefly. She and her mother were not so lucky.

Nye watched her mother as she sat by Oriana, gently caressing her daughter's hand and murmuring to her in a low voice. After more hours of close monitoring, the doctor had determined that Oriana's condition wasn't worsening. They had done all they could for her broken ribs and, as long as there continued to be no internal swelling from the head trauma, all they could do was wait. Family members were allowed to stay in Oriana's room overnight, even speaking to her, as long as they didn't do anything to excite her.

Looking at her limp sister, her unconscious mind lost in some distant place Nye didn't want to imagine, she wondered how the doctor could have possibly been concerned about excitement. No matter what they said or did, she doubted anything could disturb her sister or bring her back to life. The doctor's words had done little to convince Nye otherwise as he told them there was no time frame for the progress of this condition. Oriana could remain in a coma for hours, days, months … no one knew.

No one. Nye held onto the words. If Oriana were awake right now, she would be the first to say that God knew. If that were true, then He really was the only one to blame for this. Nye couldn't understand how a person could believe as her parents, Cullen, and Oriana did without ending up like Nye— blaming and even hating God.

As Nye watched, Mother reached out her hand and softly stroked Oriana's forehead. An image so vivid that it was almost painful sprang to life, filling Nye's vision: Mother bending over Nye's bed, caressing the forehead of her eldest daughter. Nye's young heart warmed with love and security. She was safe. She was happy.

A jolting pain from the migraine brought Nye back to the reality of the hospital room.

Her mother continued to stroke Oriana in the way she had lulled Nye to sleep so often during her childhood.

Nye ached for that time when she knew her parents loved her, and she knew God loved her—a time when love didn't hurt. He had taken so much. She had nothing left. She was finished.

She tasted the saltiness of a tear as it reached her lips. As if the tear had opened the floodgates, wet tracks burst forth and coursed down her cheeks. Her heart shattered. She bent over, sobs shaking her body. She barely felt the hand that touched her back.

"Nye? Oh, Nye." Her mother stood close, rubbing a comforting hand on Nye's back.

"Why is God doing this?" Nye's quivering lips could barely form the words between sobs. "Why would He take her?"

Mother sat in the chair next to her. "Oh, sweetie." She wiped away a tear from Nye's cheek, even as moisture welled in her own eyes. "Always the bad. Never the good. Is that what Oriana would want you to be thinking about? Sweetheart, your sister is laughter, joy ... a playful spirit. She will always be that for all of us, no matter what happens." She sniffed and looked at Oriana. "God gave me that beautiful girl, and our lives have been so blessed because of her." She turned to Nye, intense earnestness behind the tears in her eyes. "Don't lose the beauty of what you've been given because you can only see what was taken away."

Nye's tears slowed as time seemed to stand still. Something, like the beginnings of a revelation, stirred deep within. She felt as if she were on a precipice, too afraid to breathe lest she fall backward instead of grabbing onto the waiting branch above. Was that it? Was that the answer she hadn't been able to grasp? Understanding flowed as if directly from heaven, and Nye's vision began to clear.

This Dance

The Lord gives and the Lord takes away. Blessed be the name of the Lord. Russell's words from so many weeks ago echoed in her mind. She had been so focused on "the Lord takes away," that she had missed the most important part—God is also the One who gives.

How could she resent God for her pain when her sorrow only existed because His gift first brought her such incredible joy? He didn't have to let her experience so many wonderful years with Oriana. He didn't have to bring Dante into her life and let them fall in love, let them dance. God didn't have to give her any of those things, so who was she to set the time frame for His plans? What right did she have to blame Him for deciding when something else should be done with that gift? As much as Nye loved Dante, she hadn't created him. He didn't belong to her. He was God's.

As if someone had just shined a light into her soul, Nye saw for the first time the pride that had kept her away from God, away from healing. It was a ghastly sight. She didn't know when it had first started, but somehow her pride had grown until it had become the driving force of her existence. She blamed Nicanor and God for Dante's death because she thought he should have been saved. She wouldn't have let him die. She knew it wasn't right for him to be taken away.

A sour taste rose to Nye's mouth at the person she had become. Three years after Dante's death, the same pride made her resent Cullen for disrupting her life and then convinced her that she had the strength to handle a relationship with him.

She was like an unskilled dancer, always trying to seize control from the only One who could possibly lead. How ludicrous to think she could dance when she didn't know the steps, couldn't hear the music, and couldn't feel the rhythm without God revealing it to her. The result of her blind attempts to lead was only chaos, pain, and confusion. She needed God to guide her through the steps, open her ears to hear the music, and infuse her soul with His ordained rhythm.

As she clung to her mother's hand in the cold hospital room, she began to hear it … faintly at first, then louder. She heard the presence of God drawing near in a sweet melody that melted the ice around her heart and warmed the frozen recesses of her soul. As His love infused her being, a yearning grew within—a desire to sway with the music. She wanted to dance.

Happy tears tumbled down her cheeks. Now she understood what Russell had meant about wanting to remember. He didn't carry the pictures of Gary and his wife as reminders of what he had lost, but of what he had been given. Nye finally knew how Russell could quote the words of Job, and Job could speak the words he had, even after they had both lost everything. In the dismal hospital room, her soul said the words with them: Blessed be the name of the Lord.

"Nye?" Cullen's voice was hushed and laced with concern.

She looked up.

His brow was lined with worry as he stood just inside the doorway, watching them.

With the joy in her soul bubbling over, Nye leapt to her feet and rushed to him.

He caught her in his arms and returned the embrace.

She pulled back slightly and almost laughed at his astonished expression.

"What happened? Is Oriana—"

Nye shook her head. "No. She's still the same." Nye smiled, a beaming reflection of the peace and love rising from the depths of her being. "But I'm very different."

He searched her gaze. Moisture sprang to his eyes.

She sucked in a breath, overwhelmed by the happiness of the moment. "I love you, Cullen."

His eyes filled with more love than she could have imagined, and he smiled. "I love you, too."

As he lowered his head to kiss her, Nye's heart swelled with thankfulness. She had the gift of Cullen's love to cherish for as long as God intended. And it was beautiful.

Epilogue

*"And now, what does it all matter? It matters more than
anything else in the world. The whole dance, or drama, or
pattern of this three-Personal life is to be played out in each
one of us: or (putting it the other way round) each one of us
has got to enter that pattern, take his place in that dance. There
is no other way to the happiness for which we were made."*
– C. S. Lewis

"I can't tell you how happy I am for you." Oriana's eyes
glistened with emotion as she pulled back from hugging her
sister so hard Nye thought her lungs would burst.

Nye returned Oriana's watery smile with a beaming one of
her own. "I'm pretty thrilled myself." She glanced at Cullen,
who still sat at the wedding party's table, talking to Grant. A
tingle shot down to her toes at the thought that the dashing man
in the tuxedo was her husband. She felt like she had missed
most of the ceremony with her head floating in the clouds, but
she was sure it had just happened, and she was now married to
the most wonderful man in the world.

Nye turned back to Oriana. Among the blessings God had
showered upon Nye in the past six months, the healing of her
sister was the most miraculous. Three days after Nye's
relationship with the Lord was restored, Oriana came out of her

coma. She suffered no brain damage and was able to make a complete recovery. Nye thanked God every day for the gift of more time with her sister. Even this moment was precious as the two women sneaked a chance to stretch their legs and talk privately.

Oriana turned from watching Cullen with a twinkle in her eyes.

Nye braced herself for teasing as she smiled at the evidence that her sister's energetic spunk had survived.

"I don't know." Oriana's mouth slid into a sly smile. "Isn't the groom supposed to pay more attention to his bride at the wedding reception?"

Nye laughed. "Let them talk. They probably have more things to settle before Cullen leaves Grant alone at the firm." Grant had been a little nervous about Cullen going on his honeymoon when their new career move was still in its infancy.

Soon after Oriana's accident, Cullen had discovered that his re-sorted priorities made him no longer welcome at Venning and Henderson. Following God's leading, Cullen and Grant decided to establish their own private firm. The two of them worked in different areas of law, making the partnership a bit unusual, but the Lord was already rewarding their efforts to follow His plan, and the firm was doing well.

"I can understand that. Two weeks is a long time." Oriana sighed. "Two weeks in Europe. I'm so envious."

"I don't blame you." Nye's gaze was drawn back to Cullen.

He caught her watching him and winked.

Warmth surged to her cheeks. She was glad the dinner had been served and the meal was basically over. It meant she didn't have long to wait before she and Cullen would be alone.

"So who's the mysterious guy by Mom and Dad?" Oriana nodded toward the dark figure slumped in a chair.

He nodded occasionally in response to their mother's friendly attempts at conversation.

Nye couldn't help but smile at her mother's persistence, though it looked as though her cheerful efforts were wasted on the grim man.

"That's Nicanor Pessoa."

Oriana's eyes widened. "You're kidding. That's Nicanor? I didn't think he'd come."

Nye was as surprised as Oriana that Nicanor had taken her up on the wedding invitation. When he walked through the receiving line after the ceremony, he didn't even meet Nye's gaze as he muttered a basic congratulations, making her feel terrible. She was discovering that she had caused serious damage in many ways when she had turned from God.

"He's different than I pictured." Oriana still watched Nicanor.

Nye caught a look in her sister's eyes that prompted Nye to raise her eyebrows. "Too good-looking to be the man I hated?" She couldn't resist the rare chance to tease Oriana about a guy.

Oriana dropped her gaze and blushed, making Nye think she might have hit closer to the mark than she had thought. Trying to be merciful to both Oriana and Nicanor, Nye decided to rescue Nicanor from her mother. There was no time like the present for Nye to start making reparation for some of the harm she had caused.

"How was the food over here?" Nye smiled as she reached her parents' table. Russell, seated across from them, beamed as he looked up at her.

Nye's gaze met his sparkling one amid the chorus of positive responses. She had never seen him look happier. In the months leading up to the wedding, Russell had seemed more excited about the event than anyone, even though he was busy settling into the house he had purchased across the street from Nye's parents. Now, he looked positively blissful as he sat next to his daughter, Diana, and her family.

Continuing a conversation with Russell, Cullen's mother directed a smile at her new daughter-in-law. Nye responded in kind, warmed by the welcoming love with which Cullen's family had embraced her.

"You look so beautiful," Nye's father told her. "I was afraid your mother was going to start a flash flood in there during the ceremony."

Nye's mother nudged him and smiled. "I saw you shed a few tears yourself, dear." She looked at Nye. "Your father's right. You're beautiful. We're so proud of you, sweetie. So happy for you."

"Thank you." Nye smiled, her heart swelling at the sight of the pure love she saw in her parents' eyes. With the Lord's help, so much had changed since that night in the hospital. He had given her the courage to talk with her parents about her feelings, how she felt she had let them down, and dreaded their disapproval. It had taken time and understanding, but with all three of them working at it, they had started to rebuild their broken relationship.

Remembering why she had come over, Nye glanced at Nicanor, who was looking increasingly uncomfortable.

With perfect timing, Diana leaned across the table to ask Nye's parents a question, leaving Nye free to speak with Nicanor.

"Mind if I sit down?" She took his watchful silence as permission, not having expected him to answer. She pulled out a chair and sat across from him, adjusting the cumbersome folds on the skirt of her dress. Once in a somewhat comfortable position, she looked at Nicanor. "Thank you for coming."

He nodded, still avoiding her gaze.

"I wanted to apologize, Nicanor."

His blue eyes, so startling among his dark Argentine features, flitted to her face.

"For blaming you all this time. I was wrong, and I'm sorry."

He looked away. "You weren't wrong." Spoken with his slight Spanish accent, the words were barely more than a whisper.

She watched him. "I was."

He shifted in the chair, the topic clearly making him uneasy.

Taking pity on him, she dove into her next effort to make amends. "So I heard from Terry that you're between tours right now."

Though Nicanor didn't look at her, a muscle in his jaw tensed with clear irritation that his agent had called her.

"He asked me why Harper makes tango dancers want to stay and quit their careers." Nye smiled, but her attempt at humor fell flat, making her wish she had kept that bit of Terry's tirade to herself. "Not that you are quitting, of course. Probably just Terry being Terry."

No reaction. Knowing Nicanor's intensely private nature, he wasn't going to give her anything more. "I don't know if you've heard," she said, deciding to make her pitch anyway, "but I've started a dance school. I'm teaching ballet, jazz, tango. Most of the students right now are kids, and it's a lot of fun."

"I'm pleased for you. You'll do well." The sincerity in his gaze, which traveled only briefly to her face, softened his reserved tone.

"I enjoy it anyway. I wondered ... if you decide you'd like to stay here for a while, would you be interested in teaching? I could really use another instructor, and it wouldn't have to be permanent if you didn't want it to be. You'd be free to leave whenever you want."

He turned those piercing blue eyes on her for a long moment. "Why?"

She kept her expression open. "It's hard with only one teacher right now, and I hope to get more students. As I said, I need the help."

After a long pause, he pulled his hands away from where they had rested on the table and dropped his gaze. "I'll think on it."

She smiled. "Good." Nye hoped that if he agreed to her proposal he might encounter some of the joy she had found in sharing her passion for dance with others. She worried that the troubled Nicanor she knew years ago had only become more lost since Dante's death. The shadows that he carried seemed even more a part of him now, shrouding him in a darkness that was almost palpable.

"Hey, beautiful," Cullen murmured in Nye's ear.

A shiver shot down her spine with the tickle of his warm breath. She smiled as she looked up and met his loving gaze.

Cullen gently rested his hand on her shoulder and looked at the man who quietly watched them. "Hi." Cullen smiled. "Thanks for coming."

Nicanor nodded, then abruptly stood and walked away, shoving his hands in his pockets as he headed for the exit.

Cullen raised his eyebrows. "Was it something I said?"

"No. It's not you. That's his way." She watched Nicanor leave, hoping it wasn't the sight of her with a man other than Dante that caused him to go. "He just needs some space."

"Space, huh? Speaking of that …" Cullen guided her from the chair and wrapped his arms around her waist to hold her close. "What say we cut the cake and get out of here?"

She smiled. "Aren't you forgetting something?"

As if on cue, the music for their wedding dance began to play.

"Never." He grinned. "I just wanted to see if you remembered." He released her and held out his hand. "Would you like to dance?"

Looking into the loving depths of her husband's dark eyes, she smiled and responded with the passion that flooded her soul, "More than anything."

About the Author

As a writer for more than a decade, Jerusha Agen holds a Bachelor of Arts degree in English and works as a freelance editor. A long-time member of American Christian Fiction Writers, her fiction has appeared in *Graphos*, a literary journal, and she has had nonfiction articles published in various magazines and newsletters. In addition, she is a screenwriter, and several of her original  scripts have been produced as films. Jerusha is also a film critic, with reviews featured at the website, RedeemerReviews.com.

You can find Jerusha on the Web:

Redeemer Reviews – www.RedeemerReviews.com
SDG Films – www.SDGFilms.com

Look for other books

published by

www.WriteIntegrity.com

and

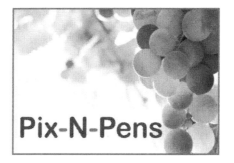

Pix-N-Pens Publishing

www.PixNPens.com